STARS ALWAYS SHINE

Bilingual Press/Editorial Bilingüe

General Editor
Gary D. Keller

Managing Editor
Karen S. Van Hooft

Associate Editors
Barbara H. Firoozye
Thea S. Kuticka

Assistant Editor
Linda St. George Thurston

Editorial Board
Juan Goytisolo
Francisco Jiménez
Eduardo Rivera
Mario Vargas Llosa

Address:
Bilingual Press
Hispanic Research Center
Arizona State University
P.O. Box 872702
Tempe, Arizona 85287-2702
(480) 965-3867

STARS ALWAYS SHINE

RICK RIVERA

Bilingual Press/Editorial Bilingüe
Tempe, Arizona

ISBN 1-931010-03-X

Library of Congress Cataloging-in-Publication Data

Rivera, Rick P.
  Stars always shine / Rick Rivera.
    p. cm.
  ISBN 1-931010-03-X (alk. paper)
    1. Mexican Americans—Fiction.   2. Male friendship—Fiction.   3. Illegal aliens—Fiction.
  I. Title.

PS3568.I8314 S7 2001
813'.54—dc21   2001025133

PRINTED IN THE UNITED STATES OF AMERICA

Cover and interior design by John Wincek, Aerocraft Charter Art Service

This is a work of fiction and verisimilitude. While characters, dialogues, and incidents might contain elements and aspects of abstract truth, they are not to be considered as real. Any resemblance to actual persons or events is, in truth, a coincidence.

For Jeannine—always for Jeannine
Also for Señor Balderas, who inspired this book
And yes, for you too, Michelle

Thanks, Mac

The land in Sonoma County, like its people, is unique. It is diverse and complex land with its flat and flush plains that buff into sinews of rippling and undulating hills, forming and hiding cells of diminutive valleys that house tiny settlements. There are mountain ridges with sharp points and steep sides, distinct as a Roman nose. A craggy, wind-worn coastline drops into the Pacific Ocean as the earth of the occident ends, and the world of the watery Orient begins many miles beyond.

There is a teeming fecundity that inhabits the land. It encourages and supports its people, who are educators, doctors, developers, lawyers, industrialists, resort operators, artisans, naturalists, people of the sea, survivalists, loggers, farmers, ranchers, and vintners. It is fertile ground that pushes up colonnades of stately, well-postured Redwood trees, pristine pine trees, thickly solid oak trees, button-wood trees dangling their clusters of seeds like gaudy jewelry, and Jack London's leaning and pungent eucalyptus trees. There are dense and deep ferns with serrated leaves reaching and twisting and coiling to coexist with the spiny vines of wild berries and forming a community with various feral plants and flowers. Poison oak melts into the vegetation, and most inhabitants know to beware leaves of three. Dancing wild grasses sway seductively in wide, open fields prompted by the susurrant music of a westerly ocean breeze, and they share their space with the flowery faces of dandelions, mustard plants, and poppies. Toward the coastal areas, pampas grass blooms in the fall, stretching its feathery white plumes skyward, protected by dense, leafy blades with edges as sharp as knives. Other botanical species are more disciplined. Uniformed rows of vineyards that produce wine grapes as light and dark as the people who walk this planet, and the fruit and elixir which make this county world renowned, stand at attention and are tended year round to ensure that what the world thirsts for is truly the best of what the earth has to offer. Many forms of garden growth thrive too; if not in the economic domain of man, then in the nutritious fullness of what nature intended. Orchards of succulent apples and plump plums pop from the buds and branches of their trees. Strawberries, blackberries, and delicate herbs flourish in the refined climate and dark, rich dirt. Fields of sweet-smelling grass hay and flaming red tomatoes grow vigorously and provide further evidence that this land is a nurturing parent.

The fauna is well represented with delegates from all points. Reclusive black bears, surreptitious mountain lions, bold wild boars, alert red-tailed hawks, sibilant rattlesnakes with their maracalike warnings, waddling possums, curious raccoons, and elegant deer reside in the underbrush and burrows and crannies that man has not yet figured out how to claim as his own. On the coast, in hard-to-reach beaches protected by buttresses and jags of cliffed rock, sea lions and their long-tusked sheiks recline and bark and flap their bodies to keep the sand fleas away. Sea otters float and bob on their backs, cracking clams on their bellies. During certain times of the year, sojourning pods of whales commute from pole to pole—some of the fancier and freer ones breaching high into the sky to show off their august bodies. And there are those whose lives depend upon the talents and sustenance of animals. Lobsters, crabs, and salmon are harvested all along the Sonoma coast. Ranchers raise capable dairy cows; breeders urge racehorses and show horses to exude their luxuriant and aristocratic blood; poultry people regulate and require eggs from legions of chickens; epicureans stuff geese and ducks to a fleshy richness; and others incarcerate calves for veal.

2

The land also has its faults—one of them as renowned as the wine. On the southwestern side of the county, extending north to south, the San Andreas fault lies in wait as it cuts its way from the ocean, grazing Valley Ford and Bodega Bay, slicing past Jenner, and reaching up into Fort Ross, Plantation, Stewart's Point, and past the coastline of adjoining Mendocino County. Geologists claim that all of this coastline is potentially receptive to the inundation of tsunami waves should the earth quake its plates substantially. Inland, another notable fault, the Rodger's Creek fault, lacerates from deep in the southern portion of the county near Sears Point and aims north for the bull's-eye of the county seat, which is Santa Rosa. In Santa Rosa, two hospitals and countless homes of healthier folks reside directly on the Rodger's Creek fault, and in that act alone, they live by faith and fate. Continuing in the same direction from there, the Healdsburg fault takes off and carves onward, running almost parallel to the main artery of human transportation, the Redwood Highway. As many as a dozen smaller, perhaps more timid, faults puncture and abrade the earth's crust, and they are all characterized as "potentially" active or "possibly" active by those who study such things.

Where the land does not slash and slit, periodic floods saturate the earth. The average annual rainfall, much of it showering down during the first few months of the year, is forty to fifty inches, and the land can only soak up so much so fast. Much of the overflowing surge comes from the tortuous and striving Russian River that meets Sonoma County in its northernmost boundary, just east of Cloverdale, and slinks southward, eventually divining its way to the receiving ocean. Numerous hamlets have attached themselves to the river like a remora to a shark. And quite often the partnership is dissolved as cresting waters remind humans who belongs where. Where the land is flat, the floods soak the fertile ground and close roads to those who live in parts of the Alexander Valley, the Santa Rosa Plain, and the southeastern portion of the county where the Sonoma Creek bursts over its banks. Other flooding of biblical proportions is offered by the Petaluma River and the south fork of the Gualala River.

In northwestern Sonoma County where the land levels flat to rolling, segments of ranch and farmland divide the earth into square portions like graph paper, with the main highway serving as the axis that distributes workers, business people, and families into tributaries of smaller windier roads that lead to individual squares and rectangles of land. The sizes of the squares and rectangles vary. Much of it depends on how a legacy has been inherited and continued, or if financial success has been attained and country living and gentleman farming becomes a goal, or simply if God's blessings have allowed for the fortunate few to live away from the humming, buzzing, pushing, pulling, crowded cacophony of city life.

Just off the center line which is the Redwood Highway, Sweet Wine Road runs parallel to the curvy influence of Miwok Creek as it marks west, then corners south, west again, abruptly south, and finally reaches for the horizon, angling west past productive farms, flowing dairies, abundant nurseries, welcoming wineries, private villas, and working ranches. On that last corner formed by south and west angles, just as Sweet Wine Road points to the setting sun and continues on to the ocean for another thirty miles, lies a sixty-acre parcel of land. And on this land rests StarRidge Ranch.

The dirt and gravel entrance draws into StarRidge Ranch off Sweet Wine Road for about fifty yards, where it is guarded by a haggard-looking, low-roofed house with loose and drooping shingles that look like bangs. It is a small, round house with its walls bulging from old age and the windowsills sagging like tired eyes. The windows are lidded with dull, tattered red cloths that might have at one time been curtains. The front door leans away from the hinged jamb and depends primarily on the lower hinge for its support. It is a loose tooth about to fall out.

The ranch road veers to the right and rises to meet a faded brown wooden ranch house sitting on a nub of ground and surrounded by a moat of dry lawns and redwood decking. Three sky-reaching pine trees stand side by side, shading the western exposure of the house. The ranch house is much bigger than the tired little guard house, and although it too needs a new roof, an enlivening coat of paint, water on the parched lawn, and some popped up and bowed boards replaced on the deck, it is the home of a landowner, a boss, a master.

The dusty course curves around the main house, and from that curve a tangent of road runs parallel to Sweet Wine Road lying alongside an antique-looking milk barn. It continues south through an open-mouthed hay barn and then proceeds on to fenced pastures of various sizes. In the midst of the fenced patches of pastures, another barn straddles the pathway dividing the ranch evenly and positioning the pastures on a sunrise side and a sunset side. Beyond this stall barn, more fenced sections dip toward Miwok Creek, which borders the eastern and southern sides of the ranch. To the west lies a much larger property— Sweet Milk Dairy—and in any direction, the closest neighbor, friend, or helper is a quarter of a mile away.

As they exited the Redwood Highway, Michelle and Plácido privately studied the segments of ranch and farmland, following the changing directions of Sweet Wine Road. Michelle and Plácido did not speak. Each pushed questions, answers, problems, and anticipations through the crevices of their brains. Michelle held the bottom of the steering wheel loosely as the murky brown truck seemed to drift along the still river of road. Plácido looked out at the open land and protective knolls, trees, and shrubs that hid the homes and lives of others. Beyond, he considered the diversity and complexity of the land.

As he viewed the passing scenes, breaking them up into individual life stories that began and ended with each demarcation of a fence or a long dirt driveway, Plácido reflected on the important events of his and Michelle's relationship. They had met in the library at Berkeley when Michelle was in law school and Plácido was just in school. He had expressed a joking sentiment about lawyers while waiting in line to check out books, and Michelle, standing behind him, took the quip as a challenge. Over coffee, she defended her profession faithfully and held up well to Plácido's cynical questions and comments. After a few quick dates and a fast marriage, they eventually finished school and settled in northern California where Michelle worked as a public defender and Plácido worked as a househusband. His master's degree in American Studies yielded little more than part-time private tutoring in the way of gainful employment.

During their eight-year marriage, they had lived modestly, first in a studio apartment in Berkeley, then in a conservative condominium in Santa Rosa. They had learned so much about each other, not having the space or private place in such small quarters to retreat to alone. And they had come, through their individual training, to respect the language of silence that each of them was fluent in.

Plácido, self-conscious and soft-spoken, had spent years working in fields and orchards. His parents had coached him that field work should be done in silence, speaking only when absolutely necessary. The important objective was to work quickly and quietly, pulling pears, plums, grapes, or cotton from their life source, placing them in buckets, boxes, or bags, and then moving on to the next tree or row. In the silent pace of mute desperation brought on by the possibilities of piecework, it was important that the eyes looked ahead. So while the hands took from one area of a vine or tree, the eyes were scanning another. For Plácido and his family, the future hung only seconds and branches away. Michelle had learned her communicative silence from working with animals, which were more responsive to soft coos, low murmurs, and caressing whispers. Especially in her years of dressage, she had learned the still and subtle cues and maneuvers that enabled her horse to understand and respond to the slightest movements of her hands and legs, and the most delicate and discreet shifts in weight. For her, this was true interaction, more than she had ever felt or known with humans.

"Are you nervous?" Plácido finally asked, now studying Michelle's profile, the strong, straight nose, self-assured jaw, and bold chin line. Her light red hair was tied back into a ponytail, and in her short-sleeved cotton blouse and blue jeans, she looked as if she belonged on this land rather than in a courtroom.

She released a reserved smile and continued to look ahead. "No. I'm not nervous at all. There's nothing to be nervous about."

"So you know what you're going to tell them?" Plácido asked, hesitated, and then added, "And what you're not going to tell them?"

"Of course I do! Our moot court last night proceeded beautifully. If you're well prepared to answer questions and you anticipate what the other side will ask, you'll do well. Don't I always win when we argue?"

"Yeah, okay," Plácido said. "But why am *I* nervous?"

"Because you want us to get this place. We decided it was time for a change and this is the perfect situation."

Michelle slowed on the last corner, and they drove onto StarRidge Ranch and past the resting cottage. Michelle took a long look at the ranch as she slowly made her way toward the house. A bright red, wide pickup truck with four wheels occupying the rear axle and ovals of orange reflectors outlining the running boards and roof of the cab was parked in front of the main house. Michelle pulled up alongside it. Before they exited their truck, she patted Plácido on the leg.

"Don't be nervous, honey. We'll do fine," she said, and her mind registered a photographic scene of the ranch before they went up to the house.

Jacqueline and Mickey Kittle sat at a kitchen table inside the ranch house. When they heard the vehicle drive up, they looked at each other. Mickey raised his eyebrows and Jacqueline rolled her eyes. There were paragraphs communicated in those expressions. Mickey's facial statement expressed a positive possibility that this interview might produce competent individuals. Jacqueline's aspect showed a hint of frustration.

He was young, in his late twenties. His wiry body and short hair exposed elfish ears, and his face was punctuated with a dot of a nose that made him look boyish. His large cowboy hat seemed too large for him, and it somehow made him look unbalanced. Mickey rose from the table and went to the front door. He was dressed for the interviews as he dressed for virtually everything else he did: the big hat, a loose and hanging T-shirt, blue jeans, and pointed, thick-heeled boots. He opened the door before Michelle or Plácido had reached it, and his kind eyes and mellow smile greeted them as he put up a hand in a waving gesture.

"Mickey Kittle," he said as he reached out to Michelle and then to Plácido. "Come on in."

The huge house was empty except for the kitchen table and chairs, which were out of place in the living room. Jacqueline remained seated as she hypnotically looked down at her yellow pad covered with inky scrawls that only ancient Egyptians might understand. Jacqueline was thirteen years older than Mickey. Mickey's sanguine attitude and easygoing manner conveyed a youthful freshness that was attractive to her, especially since her previous marriage had recently ended in a heated battle over ownership of real estate and a couple of small business holdings. At the urging of her new and young husband, Jacqueline had invested other endowed monies and sold her portion of a bar to purchase StarRidge Ranch—the name she christened it at the close of escrow. She had a prognathic jaw and perpetually down-ward-slanting eyebrows that caused the skin between them to crease vertically and which made her look as if she were always angry. Her nose sloped like a ski jump, and her thin lips glossed in a torrid crimson, matching her long, spiked fingernails, lacked passion. She wore a gingham scarf over mousy brown hair, and her double-yoked western shirt with pearl buttons and bright colors, turquoise jeans, and cowboy boots with elaborate swirls and curves made her look like a ranch owner.

Michelle reached across the table and offered her hand. "Michelle Stanton. Pleased to meet you."

"Plácido Moreno," her partner said, and offered his hand too.

Jacqueline looked up from her mesmerizing pad and said, "Oh. Hi. I'm Jacqueline Kittle." She stared at Michelle blankly for a few awkward moments before accepting her hand.

Mickey cleared his nervous throat before commencing the interview and motioned for Michelle and Plácido to have a seat. "Well, why don't we just get this thing underway?"

"I've read your resume and your letters of recommendation," Jacqueline began. "They seem to be impressive."

"Well, thank you," Michelle replied. "When I saw the ad in the paper, I thought about what it called for and what I had done years ago and what I am currently employed in, and I felt that I was as qualified as anyone around."

"Well, you do understand that the position calls for an on-site manager of this big ranch?" Jacqueline asked. "There's a lot of work on a ranch this size. But I'm sure you know that. If I asked you to go out to a pasture and halter a horse, do you think you could do it?"

"Do you have a horse and halter here?" Michelle asked. "I can go out and halter it now if you want."

Jacqueline looked away. She sublimated her surprise at Michelle's eager offer by looking over her and talking to the living room wall. "Uh, no, we don't have any horses on the place yet. We just bought it. But when we start to get some horses in, you need to be ready. We need reliable on-site people now because it will take us about a year to wrap up our business at our ranch in Woodside. Mickey is a building contractor and he has some projects to finish. I'm a trainer. We can't just walk away from our customers, you know."

"I understand what you mean, Mrs. Kittle," Michelle replied, and then asked, "What kind of a spread do you have in Woodside?"

Both Mickey and Jacqueline were caught off guard by the turn in the interview. None of the previous candidates had asked any questions and had mumbled and stuttered and sidestepped through Jacqueline's tense questioning. The couple looked at each other quickly, and Mickey said, "Well, it's a two-acre place. We've outgrew it a long time ago, and we finally decided that we needed a bigger ranch where I could do my roping and Jacqueline here could relocate her training business. This place was a steal."

Michelle, accustomed to asking questions, proceeded with another. "What kind of training do you do? English? Western?"

Jacqueline looked down at her pad and drew in a deep breath while clenching her distinct jaw. "Am I doing the interview or are you?" she asked brusquely.

"Oh! I'm sorry, Mrs. Kittle," Michelle answered, unrattled. "I just get carried away when people start to talk horses."

"She'd talk to Mr. Ed and Francis the talking mule if she could," Plácido chimed in, thinking he was witty.

Mickey laughed loudly and long. Michelle looked over at Plácido with a straight face. Jacqueline sat looking matronly and unamused.

"This one letter says you've been training out at North Coast Stables," Jacqueline said as she studied the document with a detailed letterhead of a horse running on a beach.

"That's right," Michelle said. "Benny Manfredi runs a tight ranch. I was fortunate to last with him for these past five years. Plácido has been a ranch hand on the place during those years. So the arrangement we had with Manfredi is similar to the one you're looking for." Michelle did not flinch at the lies she had delivered. It was her strategy not to reveal that she was a lawyer, anticipating that the connotation alone could render unsubstantiated images of urban sophistication and rural ignorance. And Manfredi, along with the authors of the two other thoroughly bred lies that represented letters of high praise, were quite willing to say nice things about Michelle and then sign their names to the documents in exchange for advice in wiggling out of precarious litigious situations.

The first revelation this interview yielded was that Jacqueline did not like Michelle's confidence. She cared even less for her strangely named sidekick of a husband. But having impulsively purchased a sixty-acre ranch, and not having anyone to watch and maintain it while they wrapped up business on their other property in Woodside created an urgent situation. She looked at Plácido for a few indifferent moments before asking coolly, "What kind of name is that, anyway?"

At times, Plácido was not as patient as his wife, and there was an ethnic impulse about him. References to his name were, in his mind, unsolicited references to his ethnicity, his culture, to an entire nation that helped shape and nurture California as well as other southwestern states before they were claimed by intruders. His deep blue eyes widened hatefully at Jacqueline for fleeting seconds. His high cheek bones twitched the tendons under his light brown skin as he tightened his jaw. In his mind the answer flashed, "It's an American name." But what emanated from his voice was: "It's a Mexican name, I guess. I'm Mexican American. My parents were going to name me Zeferino, but they decided on Plácido instead. People who know me call me Place."

Jacqueline remained as stoic as a statue. "Well people who know me call me Jacqueline," she said, unimpressed. Then thinking she had uncovered a flaw in Michelle and Plácido's presentation, she asked accusingly, "Didn't you two introduce yourselves with different last names?"

Under the table at which they sat, Michelle's foot lightly tapped Place's leg. She knew his anger would begin to flame as it always did when he became irritated by the conjugal question that never seemed to have any relevance to the arena in which it was presented. "Yes, we did," Michelle explained. "I'm not quite sure why you're asking, but we *are* married. I just didn't change my name when Place and I got married. Why should I?" She looked at Jacqueline with questioning eyes and a blunt expression that expected an answer.

Jacqueline shifted in her seat and raised a hand to play with the hair at the back of her neck. "Well I just find that peculiar," she said, and then diverted the discussion back to Plácido. "You say you worked on this North Coast ranch too?"

"Yes ma'am," Plácido answered politely, the tide of his anger ebbing as he remembered how badly he and Michelle wanted to live in the country, away from the urgent demands of progressive society, criminals, too-close neighbors, and door-to-door sales-people. Especially lately, because the academic world did not seem to need his intellectual talents, Place had developed a snarling attitude toward life as an argyled, elbow-patched professional and he felt a sour-graped urge to abandon the institutions that didn't want him. "I mainly mended fences, kept the barns up, made sure the waterers stayed clean, that sort of stuff," he responded, remembering from the previous night's rehearsal not to say too much and to keep things general. Plácido, as Michelle playfully teased him from time to time, was a dude. He had not had ranch exposure, even though as a young boy and before education made him more sapient and resourceful, he had worked with his parents and brothers and sisters as a migrant farm worker in Texas, New Mexico, Arizona, and California. Plácido was tremulous from the mendacity of his words. As he waited to see if Jacqueline would accept his response, he felt the same gnawing nervousness from years ago as he flashed back to his final academic act when he delivered an oral defense of his thesis, *The Pastoral Violence in the Early Writings of Hamlin Garland*. Jacqueline maintained the same severed look that Plácido received from stern professors who determined whether he had produced anything defensible.

"I guess you noticed that this place has a few barns too, and things to keep up?" Jacqueline asked both of them. Before a response came from either Michelle or Plácido, Jacqueline added, "You say Manfredi's ranch had more than one barn? It must have been about as big as this place."

Michelle answered quickly. She knew Plácido did not have the experience or knowledge to offer an impressive response. She had grown up with and around horse people and began riding when she was four years old. Michelle had ridden in Pony Club for about as many years as she went to school, and before law school, she had been certified as an instructor by the British Horsemasters Society. As an amateur, she showed and jumped horses from Pebble Beach to Fort Worth. In her bohemian days as a young, adventurous adult, she had wandered into Colorado where she eventually found work at a dairy. Achieving experience working with cattle, Michelle learned how to milk, feed, perform artificial inseminations, maintain calving and health records, and eventually, she came to manage the one thousand head of cows as she supervised a crew of a dozen milkers, feeders, and assistant managers. She knew horses, cows, and ranches as well as she knew the law. And for this interview, she was willing to risk that should she depict a convincing and complete scenario, her words alone would be enough and nobody would check her references—especially from the two who sat in the county jail awaiting their trials for nefarious horse deeds and dealings. "Oh, it was a sizable spread, Mrs. Kittle. The useable portion of the ranch consisted of a hundred acres. Then there was another sixty acres that was mainly a flood plain. We only used it to pile junk on. That ranch has a lot of the same features that this place has. Manfredi has a hay barn that will hold forty tons and a twelve-horse stall barn with automatic waterers. Two of those stalls have cameras so you can monitor your mares in foal. There is also a smaller ten-stall shed-row, a hot walker, round pen, wash rack, and a tool and hot-feed barn about the size of that little help house you have over there."

Plácido smiled deeply—to himself. He was amazed at the effectiveness of the tale that Michelle had just spun. How nicely woven, he thought. And it made Manfredi's ten-acre dirt patch, which was home to a mule that drank beer, a billy goat sexually enraptured with the mule, and dogs which were the products of an orgiastic period of random estrus, and where the roofless barn was almost in as good a condition as his house, seem so well kept, so organized, like something he imagined would be in Kentucky next to Churchill Downs.

Jacqueline Kittle sat and stared. She was unaware that Michelle's narrative had impressed her enough to cause her mouth to drop open, weighted wide by her heavy jaw, while her brain tried to figure out things like hot walkers and shed-rows and round pens.

Michelle, highly trained in body language, human nature, and the subtle, silent gestures and expressions that say so much, knew when and how to take advantage of such things.

"Of course, Mr. and Mrs. Kittle, I realize that Plácido and I might not be qualified to meet your standards, and I realize too that you have other applicants to interview. We're just extremely grateful for the opportunity to have this interview. Fortunately, we have another one tomorrow at a ranch in Napa County." Michelle was now appealing to her jury of two, and the same energizing force began to consume her when she knew toward the end of a trial that she had delivered a convincing final argument. She had honed her professional presentations to include analogical paradox, curious understatement, and tacit accusations. Jacqueline Kittle sat pricked with the subtle acupuncture of words.

But Jacqueline was a fighter too, albeit an already beaten one. And it was really only black-eyed pride that forced her to answer the bell for another round of this rhetorical bout. "Why are you leaving Manfredi?" she asked.

The thoughts rotated and flashed in Michelle's mind like a kaleidoscope. There were so many options at this point with respect to answering such a simple question. She scrolled through the citations in her brain as she thought about how long to continue this exchange, in what direction to lead the interview, and what would really win the Kittles over.

"Manfredi's dying," she said as she looked deeply into Jacqueline's eyes and knowing that at most, Manfredi might be drunk and passed out in his hammock. "He's had so much radiation pumped into him, he probably glows at night. He really doesn't have much longer. Maybe a year at most. We offered to stay with him, but his children are going to help with the ranch now."

"I'm sorry," Mickey whispered, now hunched over in his seat with his elbows on his thighs, looking down, pursing his lips, and shaking his head from side to side at the brutal indignation of life.

"Yes, that's too bad," Jacqueline said regarding the wall she seemed to have grown fond of.

"But please, do call him if you wish to talk to him," Michelle said. "Or better yet, go by his ranch. Since I presume you aren't too familiar with the county, I can give you directions to his place. He is still strong enough to get around and talk to people."

Place regarded Michelle admiringly. He recognized that she was now presenting her case in what he referred to as her out-of-body mode, or as a woman possessed. She had done that over coffee in their initial conversation at Berkeley. She did this at home whenever they got into arguments. And she thrived on it in the courtroom. It was her talent to drive the main points home and then keep driving them into the foundation while adding bits and pieces of other details, comments, and developments until they overwhelmed or confused or frustrated. He wondered how much more she would bring into the exchange, but he did not have to wonder much longer.

"How much irrigation do you need to do a day?" Michelle asked. "I understand that the North County Irrigation District requires ranchers and farmers in this area to use up a certain amount of tertiary treated water each day. What does your contract with them call for?"

Jacqueline turned quickly to Mickey, who sat up straight after his mourning for Manfredi. She hesitated, coughed, cleared her throat and replied, "Uh, well, now that's a very good, uh, question you ask, Michelle, we understa—."

Michelle was now successfully surfing the discursive pipeline of churning words and feeling the exhilaration of such an experience. She interrupted to calmly offer, "Please, Mr. and Mrs. Kittle, call me Mitch. He's Place and I'm Mitch. At least down at Manfredi's and at the feed store and with the shoer and the vet." She smiled in a heavenly way at Mrs. Kittle and then at Mickey. She knew that the advantageous position of being the least ignorant one in a conversation usually made the other grope and flinch and squirm. She sat demurely but with postural aplomb as she waited for an answer.

"To be honest with you, Mitch, we aren't sure," Mickey revealed, the huge hat on his small head making him look like a disproportionate caricature. "The real estate agent just sold us this place so quick, we didn't have much time to figure a lot of things out or ask many questions." He was sheepishly embarrassed at the thought of having his wife pay half a million dollars for a piece of property thirty times bigger than anything either one of them had ever owned without finding out the details. But that was what moved Mickey—not knowing the details. Details got in the way of those other things Mickey had his sights on. Becoming a cowboy and working his own ranch were simple enough goals in his mind. Why should they be complicated with details?

Jacqueline tried to ease the growing flush both of them were increasingly feeling as the room languished in an uncomfortable silence. "We will be going to the county offices tomorrow to research those vital issues," she said, using words that seemed to exceed her true intelligence. Then abruptly, to ease her annoyance, she decided the interview was over. She stood to indicate such, and thanked Mitch and Place for their time. "We'll call you within a week to let you know the results," she said.

As they left the ranch, Place waved to the little round house. They drove down Sweet Wine Road, following the right angles toward the Redwood Highway. Place and Mitch stared out at the exposed land as they quietly drifted home. He thought about those individual parcels of private lives that were supported, encouraged, and motivated by the earth. Without announcing it, Mitch took a side road, delaying the inevitable hubbub of the Redwood Highway, and drove deeper into the honeycombs of valleys to visit land she had come to miss. After silent minutes of wandering through various shades of green, Mitch accelerated as she merged with the ambitious traffic of the highway.

"That was brilliant, honey!" Place said, reviewing what had taken place in the interview. "Are you sure you don't want to continue practicing law? I know you're burned out, but you really have a talent for twisting, bending, spindling, stretching, and contorting the truth and other facts. Simply brilliant!"

"Oh, it was nothing, really nothing," she said with a huffed tone of dispassionate refinement. Then changing her tone to one of serious concern, she added, "They'll call within two days, maybe even tonight to let us know we have the position. Something's not right with those two. There is something peculiar about this whole situation. And I'm not talking about their obvious age differences. You don't go into this kind of a property uninformed. It appears that they didn't look into things before they committed to buying the place. Probably because there's a lot to read and it's easier to just look at something and say, "I want it." It's kind of late to be researching things now. Yes, that ranch does need a whole lot of work, but the fencing alone is worth tens of thousands of dollars. That's not a casual investment. Let's just get home to see how Rosa is doing and wait for their call."

The phone rang early the next day. Before Mitch picked up the receiver, she was confident that Jacqueline Kittle would be on the other end of the conversation. She hesitated for a few seconds while she gathered her thoughts and answered, "Good morning, North Coast Stables, this is Mitch speaking."

Jacqueline Kittle, despite not really liking Mitch and Place, was impressed with the professional tone. She had no reason to suspect that her words, after being spoken into the receiver and traveling with electric speed through wires, cables, and transformers, reached their destination not at Benny Manfredi's allegedly bucolic ranch, but instead found a home in Mitch's ear in a metropolitan condominium only walking distance from the county administration complex where she really worked.

"Mitch, we'd like to have you over for another interview. We've narrowed the applicants down to three, and you're one of them."

Jacqueline and Mickey did not have any other applicants. Their three days of interviewing produced candidates who either wanted more money, more amenities, fewer working hours, or a combination of those requests. In Jacqueline's mind, all of the applicants had been frauds, ne'er-do-wells, and parasites.

Mitch wanted to keep her bargaining chips stacked high. She informed Jacqueline that they still had to consider their options should they be given a position at their fictitious interview in Napa county. She knew who was capable of what in Sonoma county's horse world, as most of her associates and acquaintances were ranch owners, trainers, veterinarians, jockeys, grooms, horseshoers, and horse traders, so she was not concerned with the competition that Jacqueline Kittle spoke of. In addition, Mitch trained beginning riders and rode on weekends at a busy equestrian facility, and she knew talk on ranches was akin to linguistic brush fire—it spread rapidly.

"Well, I'll be honest with you, Mitch," Jacqueline revealed, "As far as I'm concerned, you are the top one of the three. Mickey feels the same way too. I just need to interview the others because I've already called them back for another interview. I can guarantee you the job's yours. You can take that as a verbal contract."

"I'm flattered, Mrs. Kittle. But you know, a verbal contract is as good as the paper it's written on. We need more assurance than that. I'll tell you what. Go ahead and interview your other two people and we'll go interview at Napa and let's just let nature take its course. How does that sound?"

Mitch could not see the deep shade of red that roiled up on Jacqueline's face, creating a burgundy blush. She could not see the clasped jaw or the creases in Jacqueline's forehead that became more pronounced. But she savored the gelid nonchalance that she could only imagine discomfited Jacqueline Kittle.

"That's fine, Mitch," Jacqueline answered as she rebounded from frustration. "Can you make it the day after tomorrow? We need to get back to Woodside in a few days, and we'd really like to have things in order. Oh yeah, does Place speak Spanish?"

"Why, yes he does," Mitch answered curiously.

"I need him to help me with something when you come over," Jacqueline explained, not offering further details.

Mitch hung up the phone. As she turned, Place loomed behind her as quiet as a wooden Indian. Startling her into taking a quick step back, he grabbed her forcefully, drawing her body snugly into his and kissing her as if it were the last kiss or the first.

"Are you bending somebody's mind with your barrister's language?" he asked. "And so early in the morning."

She leaned her face back as Place continued to hold her close. "They want us to come back for another interview. We're going to get to move onto that ranch, I know it! I can get a horse again. I can teach you how to ride. And they won't be around too much."

They hopped around the living room as they held onto each other, dancing a silly dance and laughing. Rosa watched curiously, the lively movement exciting her to almost the same hopping dance. They bounced over to the couch, falling onto it, and Place pushed his body into Mitch's as he lay on top of her. His hands roamed down to her waist, pulling at her nightgown as he kissed her hard. His face nuzzled into the nest of flesh just under her jaw and down to her neck.

"Place," she whispered seductively, "we can't."

"Don't tell me," he whispered back, "it's that time of the month, huh?"

"Yes," she said, "I have to be in court early today."

osa the Airedale stood boldly in the bed of the pickup as it drove onto StarRidge Ranch. She had not seen much more than the tidy neighborhood park with its orderly lawns and trees that had a plastic appearance to them and were planted in clean dirt squarely bound by neatly placed boards. She had spent all except the first two months of her five years in the sterile condominium that provided nothing more in the way of outdoor experience than the walled and cement enclosure of the small patio.

The ranch excited Rosa. It challenged her. It called to her. There was a myriad of mysterious smells, and they provoked her to explore each and every one. Her nose floated upward as she took periscopic whiffs of horse manure, cow manure, mildewing hay, the fresh scent of trees, and the dry smell of dust. Her coal-like eyes, set deep in curly reddish fur, scanned the ranch as she breathed in the canine's mother lode.

She was Mitch and Place's only dependent. Before they married, they had peaceably agreed that they would have no children. In a way, they were still youthful and did not feel capable of molding the personality of another human being. So they agreed that animals would be as far as their parentage would extend, and Rosa was their first. The three traveled together up and down the state on camping trips, hikes in the mountains and woods, to Disneyland where there is a kennel, to rivers, lakes, and the ocean where they all jumped in and splashed about. But those outings were always too short and impermanent. And while Mitch practiced law, Place washed, brushed, and took Rosa to the vet, to the groomer, and to the park.

Once, Mitch and Place decided that Rosa should have her own family, so they bred her to a champion Airedale. Just exactly what he was a champion of was never clear, but he was beautiful and could pose like an Adonis. He sired five healthy pups who had purebred conformation. It was a trying pregnancy for Place, who made sure that Rosa was comfortable and well nourished during her gestation. But the addition of five terrier puppies drove Place to such vigilant nervousness that he decided that there would not be another litter after this one was sold. Rosa's puppies did sell for impressive figures, and it made the puppy business appear lucrative, but it was frustrating living with them in a now cramped home and always looking for things like underwear, a belt or cap, or a favorite pen. The condition of motherhood soon evaporated from Rosa, and once again the family returned to a cohesive unit that could lie around the house and watch television without a smaller, more exploratory terrier chewing and teething on the leg of a chair or a shoe or an umbrella.

Rosa had not grown as a member of her human family as much as Mitch and Place had become members of her canine pack. Together, they were alpha, beta, and gamma dogs. And their bond had even inspired Place to write poetry. He worked sedulously one day creating an ode to his dog Rosa:

> We have a dog, a curly haired mutt,
> With curls from her head all the way to her butt.
> Her vet bills are high, if she talked she'd say ouch;
> That is except when she jumps on the couch.
> What's the breed of this dog? Oh, she's an Airedale,

And now that I remember, she has a malodorous smell.
She's the dog of the house, and we love her dearly,
But her passion for the couch runs from acute to severely.
She is our dog; she has captured our hearts,
And armed with incense, we tolerate her farts.
So here's to our dog, who barks and does snore.
We ask very little, and she gives us no more.

Of course others found the human and animal relationship a little strange, but Mitch and Place jokingly explained that they simply got along better with four-legged animals than with upright primates who spoke English. And they were grateful after a session of honest and earnest negotiating that Jacqueline and Mickey Kittle allowed them to have a pet on the sixty-acre ranch.

The transformation occurred in a flash. Rosa the condominium dog became Rosa the ranch dog in the time it took her to jump from the back of the moving pickup to pursue a flock of bobbing blackbirds who poked and jabbed at the lawn where hints of green remained. The birds flew away, squawking back mockingly at such effrontery.

Place and Mitch casually called Rosa, certain that their commands of "Rosa, come," and her weeks of private puppy obedience school, where she earned her degree as a "Pawticularly Good Dog," would cause her to decelerate and return immediately to the truck. But the gamma dog did not listen to her pack leaders. She ran down the dirt roadway continuing on to the stable barn and through it, and down to the sloping pastures that ended at Miwok Creek. She slinked flat through a gap between the earth and fence and ran in a serpentine fashion along and in the creek, chasing nothing but being grasped and pulled along by the allure and freedom of open, fragrant, authentic land.

efore Jacqueline and Mickey Kittle left StarRidge Ranch under the management of Mitch and Place, they discussed the job duties and wages. Place tried to pay attention, but he was distracted by the thought that Rosa had not returned to the ranch. His hours of searching for her had produced no wandering Airedale. He listened, but his mind was on his lost dog and not on his newfound home.

Mitch and Place would live in the big ranch house for one year. In addition, the couple would receive a modest check for working six days a week. In exchange, regular ranch chores had to be carried out. More specifically, the eighteen pastures had to be irrigated on a rotating schedule, but daily. The lawns had to be brought up to a satisfying green too. Barns had to be cleaned and operational, and as an immediate impression, the fence that encircled the entire property had to be painted to its original bright white, as did the shelters in each of the pastures. There were no horses to take care of, but Jacqueline promised that the first pasture tenants would be hers and Mickey's horses and some other animals they owned. As soon as possible, they would open up the ranch as a boarding facility. While they discussed the game plan and guidelines, Mitch documented as much as she could by taking notes on a yellow legal pad.

Mitch wrote quickly, scribbling notes in the margins in addition to what Jacqueline Kittle had explained, ordered, and demanded: "Jacqueline is in charge," and "Check with title company to see whose names are on the deed," and "Mickey's along for the ride—will stay on for as much as he can get out of the place and Jacqueline!" It had become clear to Mitch that the true owner of the ranch, in spite of whose names she might find on the deed, was Jacqueline. Mitch could see that Jacqueline was accustomed to being in charge; she owned things and that could include individuals in the arrangement that was Jacqueline Kittle's private universe. That meant that eventually, when the markers were called in, people owed Jacqueline in many ways and with their hearts and souls, whatever it was that she felt made things even.

"We're going to be here next week to see how things are going," a smiling Jacqueline said. She had relaxed considerably now that she knew her ranch would be occupied and fixed up. But there remained a miasmic aura about her that she wore like a thin silk shroud. Her smile never broke into a clean, honest smile—the kind that brightens a face and sets the eyes like starlight. There was always something, perhaps from her history, that suppressed the upward turns of her mouth. With Jacqueline, one could reach out and seemingly palpate her disposition as if feeling a swatch of material. "But don't worry, we won't invade your precious home—just remember, if it wasn't for us, you'd be out on the street, you know. We're going to camp out in one of the barns. Stuff like that is easy for country folks like us. Now, I need Place to help me out with something. There's a guy that lives in that shack, and I want you to tell him he has to be gone in three weeks."

Place and Mitch were surprised, and they showed it as their expressions formed questions.

"You mean somebody is actually living in that house?" Mitch asked.

Place was puzzled. "Who is he?"

"He's some Mexican," Jacqueline replied. "When we bought this place, the owners told us that they wanted to let this guy stay on for another month until he found work someplace else. They said he was the best worker they had, even though he doesn't speak any English. When this property was full of horses, it was a big thoroughbred ranch, and there were a lot of ranch hands who lived and worked here. I guess that was like a bunkhouse. You know, at one time, this ranch had almost two hundred horses on it!"

Mitch had heard about the reputation of StarRidge Ranch when it was Thundering Thoroughbreds Ranch. She also knew that the world of racehorses could be a cruel and expensive business. Eventually the cost of running such a facility caught up to and passed the owners, who sold out and fled just before creditors could claim their due. Of course, it was a hot item of discussion in the local horse world, and the "do-tell" and "you-don't-say" talk was usually pretty reliable information.

Jacqueline continued, "They paid us for his rent, so we made a few dollars out of the deal. But we want him out of here as soon as his time's up."

"So you're not thinking of keeping another hand on?" Mitch asked. "If he was good enough for the previous owners to care about, and good enough to stay on at what was once a major thoroughbred facility, he would probably be valuable to keep around for awhile. He knows the ranch better than any of us. And he could certainly help with the irrigation."

"That's a thought," Mickey said. "We know we need to off twenty-five hundred gallons of water a day, but we really don't know the irrigation pattern."

"No. I just can't pay another worker," Jacqueline countered. "Mickey and me can help out on weekends. The four of us can run this ranch. We'll just have to wing it for awhile. Just tell him to leave in three weeks."

"Well, didn't the previous owners tell him when he had to be gone?" Place asked.

"Yes, they did," Jacqueline answered impatiently. "But I want you to tell him just to remind him. We're going to remodel that place and rent it out. We need the extra income. Like I said, the guy can stay until his rent's up, but we've got to get moving on bringing this entire ranch up to working condition. I can't have no dead weight around here. I'm sorry if that sounds cruel, but business is business."

Mitch and Place watched and relaxed as the flashy red pick-up left them and StarRidge Ranch in quiet coexistence. They held each other's waists as they turned and took in the panorama of their new home. At the end of Place's circle of view, he was reminded of the message he had to deliver as the small, worn help house signaled to him.

"Well, you better go talk to the guy, honey," Mitch said. "I'm going in to finish up the last bit of work I have left before I'm cut loose from the office and make arrangements to have the condo rented." She was happy that she no longer would have to interpret the law and argue for issues that often conflicted with her own ethos.

"I hope he understands my Spanish," Place said to himself as he walked to the house which he had always presumed was uninhabited and uninhabitable.

Place approached the house slowly. He was running various phrases of Spanish through his head to tune up for the conversation. He did not speak Spanish as often as he would like to. When he did meet someone who spoke that other language, he would try to start a conversation as best he could. But usually Place's words became a bilingual salt and pepper seasoning that only worked with those like himself, those whose own minds tried to negotiate the rhythms and verb tenses of Spanish with an English that was inherently mezclado, all mixed up. He regretted that one of the sacrifices in advanced education, and in all formal education, was giving up that other language, and with it that other culture that periodically returned to him in singing medleys and rhythmic movements and laughing playfulness. Yet in his head, while meeting the demands of one who would be considered educated, he tried to assume the serious, impersonal, linear, and analytical tone of words that seemed to move around stiffly and awkwardly, unrestrained words that used up the entire dance floor of paper in twirling and rocking patterns and tried to polka when he needed them to waltz.

He understood Spanish much more than he spoke it. And when he did speak it, Place's Spanish was a curious mixture of school-taught Castilian Spanish in which he always enrolled to earn an easy A; home-spoken Chicano Spanish mixed with English and using words from both languages to form the bicultural expressions with which he was most familiar; and a spicing of Argentinean Spanish that he picked up during his year as a vagabond in Central and South America, where he settled for six months when he had left the United States in his late teens because a girlfriend had broken up with him. At that time, he had sworn off American women and decided his heavy heart needed a change. Going south, he had reasoned, would be like returning to an archetypal home and mother.

He slowed his pace as he rehearsed his salutation and thought of the most tactful way to deliver his message. He looked down at the ground as he mumbled words and phrases, some of which did not sound right to him or sounded clumsy.

The front door was as closed as it could be as it hung from its frame. There were streaks of light at the top, bottom, and sides of the door where it did not close flush. Place knocked carefully, and the door swayed lightly in many directions.

A short, stout, dark man pulled the door in and staring at Place, jerked his head upward to ask with that gesture what his order of business was. His face was round, like a jack-o'-lantern's and later when he smiled, Place would see that his teeth were just a little more substantial than the ones cut into a traditional jack-o'-lantern's scary grin. His hair streaked forward and fell flat on his forehead as if an invisible cap smashed it down. His eyes were dark and big, like a frightened animal's eyes, and the horizontal red lines that mapped the whites of them completed a ghastly and jaded expression.

Place studied him carefully. He looked at the man and saw more than his moon-round face. He saw the many faces of the weary field workers he had seen as a boy. It was that once familiar expression of futility that never quite defeated a person like this, but poked and prodded at him just enough to scratch a festering and cynical indifference toward life.

Place gulped slowly and began. "Buenas días. Cómo e—"

The big-eyed man interrupted him curtly to correct, "¡No! No es día, es tarde. Y no es buena con día, es bueno. Buenos días o buenas tardes."

Place looked at him with surprise and managed a profound "Oh." He gathered himself and tried again, this time telling himself to concentrate on what he had just learned and felt he should have already known. "Buenas tardes. ¿Cómo estás?" he started out safely, measuring each syllable metronomically.

"Fine. Thank you," the man answered with a shrilled accent that exuded effort in careful expression as much as response.

Place soured his face in confusion. "Do you speak English?" he asked.

"No. And you?"

"Well, yes," Place began, and then chuckled nervously as he realized the incipient conversation was not making sense.

The dark man laughed at Place's twisted face and offered, "I speak little bit English. Poquito." And he held up a hand with his index finger and thumb narrowly separated to indicate his limited second language. "What you name?" the dark man asked.

"Plácido Moreno," Place replied with a fine, ornate accent. He reached out toward the man.

"¿Plácido Moreno, eh? Salvador Campos. Mucho gusto." He accepted Place's smooth, clean hand with a scabrous and solid grip, and then he invited Place into his home.

The cramped living room had a single couch squatting in it with one of its two cushions missing. One remaining faithful cushion bulged with padding, pushing up through a gushing tear. Next to it, a renegade metal spring spiraled upward from the base of the couch. As Place stepped into the living room, a white tailless cat ricocheted into another part of the house. Straight back from the living room was a small kitchen. There was an old enameled white and rusted stove with a smaller camp stove placed directly on top of it. A small wooden table stood a few feet from the stove, and there was a solitary milk can positioned close to the table to indicate that this was where the diner sat. The limited kitchen window looked out to an unpainted wooden wall which Place would later find out was the side wall to Salvador's outhouse, as his house had no functional toilet. Rays of light leaked through the roof where the short hallway led to a tiny boxlike bedroom.

Place sat tentatively on the edge of the couch thinking he might become infected by something. He pinched at his nose repeatedly and wiped his upper lip to help his nostrils battle the thick mustiness that hung heavily in the living room. He delivered Jacqueline's message and waited for Salvador's response, which was one of understanding as he nodded his head and said, "Sí, yo sé." The previous owners had already explained the situation to him, and Jacqueline had days earlier tried to reinforce the same message but only in English and with primitive hand signs. He was well aware of his time and his rights, and he told Place this.

Aside from the intended business, Place was as curiously interested in Salvador as Salvador was in him. They asked each other tentative questions about where they came from, where they had been, and where they were going.

Place gave his story first. With intense concentration, he explained in a jerky, bucking Spanish, which Salvador patiently coaxed out of him and corrected, that his parents were from Mexico and he had been born in the Imperial Valley in Southern California. He had nine brothers and sisters who were born in various other valleys and lived in different states. He told Salvador that he had lived in many towns, had gone to many schools, and had picked many types of fruits and vegetables. He also left out many details, not wanting to reveal his entire existence in this initial encounter and not feeling comfortable talking about himself.

Diverting the discussion from himself to Salvador, Place's first question was an abrupt "¿Eres legal?" He wasn't sure why he asked this. His own father had never taken the time to become a legal citizen of the United States, and the family never concerned themselves with the issue. It was something everyone, including labor contractors, took for granted or didn't want to know about in the first place. Citizenship was not a prerequisite to doing work that legal citizens did not want to do or felt by their birthright that they should not have to do.

Salvador recognized that Place could be Mexican; his name indicated that. But Salvador could see and hear that Place was distinctly more American. And as the opposition of thoughts collided in his mind, Salvador wondered if he could trust Place. The Mexican part of Place merited cultural and ethnic allegiance. The American part of Place could bring with it uglier things, the things many Americans felt about immigrants and immigration, like meddling officiousness, misguided indignation, and maybe even meaningless envy.

Salvador looked at Place dubiously. He wondered who this culturally filtered and watered-down Mexican was. He knew only too well that Americans employed legal Hispanics to work for them as spies for la migra. But it also did not make sense that Place asked a single individual. It was always preferable to catch a whole bunch of illegals—like trapping rabbits—and then set them free in the wilderness of their own country where they belonged.

"No. Soy ilegal," Salvador answered unflinchingly, looking at Place with recalcitrant eyes.

"¿Mojado, huh?" Place responded.

"¡No!" Salvador said, adding a tone of denial to his expression. "Mojado, no. Alambrado."

Place was bewildered. From his prior knowledge, as he had been told his father had done, he assumed that the illegal point of entrance for those who migrated south to north was made by swimming across the river; that was how the term "wet" or "wetback" was explained to him by older brothers. He had also assumed that even if someone crossed into the United States through California, Arizona, or parts of New Mexico where there is no river to wet one's back, there was still a wetness or aspect of being mojado and thereby illegal.

Salvador, understanding the jumbled expression his response created, read Place's confusion. He explained to him that if one crosses over into Arizona, say, as he had, one would have to cross over, under, or through a wire fence or a fence made of alambre. So the correct term was *alambrado*. Once he prepositionally made it past the wire fence, Salvador told Place as he shifted his explanation to the story of his arriving, there were miles and miles of desert to cross, and the crossing had to be made on "la carretera del diablo," the dangerous Devil's Highway. "Es muy peligroso," he warned Place as if some day he would take such a journey. He saw human skeletons in the desert as he worked his way to a secret meeting point where he was transported north in the trailer of a furniture truck with a few dozen other paisanos. Three flesh-baked and thirsty days later, he was in Washington state picking apples. From Washington, the truck smuggled the work crew down to Oregon, and from Oregon down to the Sacramento Valley and then over to the abundant vineyards of Sonoma county.

In Mexico, Salvador continued as he wound his way backwards with a brief autobiography, he had worked with his family's few cattle and attended school when he was not attending to his devoted mother and useless father. But he did finish his education all the way through the eighth grade, he added with a flourish of pride. And sensing that Place or most people who looked at him saw only an ignorant immigrant, Salvador stated, "No soy estúpido. No más tengo la cara."

Salvador laughed and waited for Place to understand his joke. Salvador also revealed that he had worked at racetracks near the frontera because the border and what lay north of it interested him. He slept in stalls and cared for horses whose lives seemed to be worth more than his own. He knew horses, but he did not know the other side of the fence. On the day he thought was his birthday—he wasn't sure about the exact day, and he really was only close on his exact age, but time was abstract and subjective anyway, he explained, and much more of a concern to Americanos as was money—he made the crossing with a memorable hangover, a modest savings, a jug of water, and a package of corn tortillas.

One day when he was walking back to his culvert that ran under a bridge and into Miwok Creek, and which was home to him and a few others, Salvador exhibited to the owners of Thundering Thoroughbreds Ranch his talent with horses when he caught a high-strung thoroughbred that had escaped, and rode it onto the ranch bareback using his belt as a halter. He left the culvert for the small help house which he shared with three other ranch hands and worked full-time and year round.

He didn't want to leave the ranch that had been his home for almost two years. He didn't want to go back to Mexico, but he had no idea where he would be going. He told Place that he had petitioned Jacqueline and Mickey for work by gesticulating shoveling motions, raking movements, and lifting pantomimes, but they declined the request. Then he scoffed and predicted that Jacqueline and Mickey would not be able to run the ranch successfully. He could see it in their movements. Their movements were awkward, too slow and stiff, and they didn't know as much about the land as the animals did. They were like lost foreigners. He added emphatically, "¡Aquí, *ellos* son ilegales!"

"But what about your family?" Place choppily asked with Salvador's linguistic assistance.

"¿Mi familia? No tengo familia. Hermanos y hermanas, sí, en México, pero no tengo esposa ni hijos," Salvador explained as he threw in an editorial comment on the challenging economics of having a family. "Esposa y niños cuestan mucho. No más tengo mi gatita." He then asked who would be working on the ranch, and when Place told him only himself and Mitch, he presumed that there would be no horses on the property.

But yes, there would be horses, Place told him. The owners wanted to fill all of those empty pastures. A monthly mortgage had to be met. StarRidge Ranch was destined to be a working and bustling horse ranch just as it had been in its previous life.

Salvador explained that in that case, the ranch would need more workers. The work required could not be done by only a couple of full-time ranch hands—no matter how industrious they were. The irrigation alone took up to three hours because of the necessity of moving and setting the water hoses; sometimes a hose would burst holes that needed to be patched. And the hoses that came with the ranch when the Kittles purchased it were well past their prime. Sprinklers and couplers had to be reattached or repaired with regularity. And then there was the daily mucking out of stalls. The barns needed to be cleaned, and the waterers needed to be scrubbed and disinfected at least once a week. Horses had to be moved to other pastures or to holding pens for one reason or another, especially when the rains came and there were horses in those lower pastures out back—they would flood. Occasionally a horse needed to be held for a vet or a shoer. Other occasions required that pastures be turned and replanted or they became overgrazed and the weak grass would have no nutritional value. Weeds had to be sprayed. Not to mention the general upkeep of the landscaping—look at how bad the lawns were—and the usual fixing of things always used up the valuable hours of a work day. No, this ranch could not be effectively worked by someone merely infatuated with labor. And even if you think you are holding up well to the demands, it takes its toll. It runs a man down. It slowly breaks his spirit. That's why it is so hard to find reliable workers. This type of work forces you to look for something else. To move on. Only those who are desperate and illegal can manage. And quite often, the desperate become confident and find something easier, and the illegal go home.

Place was stunned. He hadn't realized what was required to make a setting so pastoral looking. Doesn't Mother Nature take care of most of those things? he wondered naively. Then he remembered that Salvador had not even referred to all of the painting that Jacqueline and Mickey wanted done. He bid Salvador a good evening and with a nervous concern walked up to the faded ranch house.

There are always cats on a ranch. Ranch cats survive well enough on their own. They are adept in their masterly ways when they hunt for mice in barns and crouch patiently with the silence of an assassin, waiting to pounce on gophers that push up through the earth. They are a low-maintenance animal, hearty as the land and deft as a secret breeze.

Salvador's little cat, Gatita, was quite able as a hunter, but she was different, as cats go, in her companionship. Her markings were unusual, as she was mostly white with black splotches on her underside. Her chin was streaked with a black stripe that traveled down her neck and ended where her legs began. On her head she wore a spattered cap of black. But what was really unique about this cat is that she followed Salvador around as a dog follows its master. She heeled without being taught how to do so. She even seemed to walk like Salvador, taking the same quick, deliberate strides that did not waste time when work was abundant and the day always seemed too short. With Salvador, she did not display that aloof and coy lack of concern that most cats tease their owners with. While Salvador worked in a pasture or cleaned a barn, Gatita waited close by, often sunning herself

37

in the sleep-inducing solar light or stretching thin and licking herself clean. When anybody approached, she would slither off into hiding, but she always remained in close proximity, watching Salvador.

The morning after Place and Mitch had settled into their new home, Salvador told Place the story of his Gatita as he offered a walking tour of the ranch. Place listened attentively, even though he was distracted and mildly depressed about losing Rosa. Salvador had saved his little cat after almost stepping on her when he had found her in a barn one cold morning. Her eyes were newly opened, and she pushed along the ground trying to go where only destiny led. He laughed when he said that she moved more like a sea turtle on a beach. Her small legs were limp, and crawling was still beyond the scope of her development. Salvador searched for a mother. He listened for mewing babies that might signal that it was time to be fed. He called out the high-shrilled and rapid cry that some cats respond to. He asked others if they knew who this kitten could belong to, and he found himself holding a tiny creature who had no mother and no tail.

During his lunch break that day, Salvador rode his bicycle to the little market down the road and purchased some milk. He placed the milk in a bowl, and the bowl in a box with the weak kitten. Gatita did not have the instinct to lick the milk from the bowl because she would still be suckling from a mother's teat if one were available. That evening as Gatita lay helpless, Salvador made an urgent trip to a farther but much bigger store and purchased a baby bottle. He carefully held the little cat in one hand as he poked the nipple toward her mouth. The nipple of the baby bottle was too big for Gatita's puckered mouth, but she managed to take some fluid in while most of it ran down her face and neck. One day, as Salvador was administering a healthy shot to a sick horse, he looked at the large syringe as he slowly pushed the medicine down through it and into the needle. Struck with ingenuity, he imagined the syringe without the needle dispensing a controlled dose of milk to his baby cat. Before work, after work, and during his lunch break, Salvador nurtured his kitten with a syringe of milk. She grew quickly, maturing into a competent mouser and an even more capable companion.

Cats are, for the most part, nocturnal. Gatita, as unusual as she was, was no different. Salvador respected this, and he wedged a beer can between the front window of his cottage and the sill to allow his cat to respond to the nightly callings as the urge demanded.

In the night, other living beings come out too. The stillness of the slowly moving water in Miwok Creek, the leaning trees that drape a shadowy shroud along the banks, and the thin fog that rises from it like a long, gasping breath, harbor a night life of stealthy ambition as creatures awaken and seek out warm bodies that would be nourishment for their own families. It is a place that requires one to walk deftly and alertly, and still others are always watching and waiting.

They were prehensile claws that ripped into the silent night air and with a swift force seized the curious cat and lifted it from the muddy bank. The cat's initial shriek was devoured by the stifling fog as it twisted its body and flailed at the ascending creature in a desperate effort to pull itself free from the clutching and crushing power. The round, feathered body swooped low as it wavered out of control. Slamming into the murky ground, the fierce talons automatically spiked into its prey and weighed heavily on its capture as it tore at the struggling, squirming feline. The hooked claws lacerated fur and flesh like a slitting gust slashing through the thick air.

From behind the slaughtering animal came a low but vicious growl, and then a tearing sensation at its neck as it cleaved at its own victim. The three-linked struggle rolled and reeled in the savage chaos of the dark and turbid landscape. The quiet waters of Miwok Creek broke the feral silence with desperate thrashing splashes that muffled the squeals and yelps and cries.

A hideous screeching shriek hit threatening high notes and evaporated into the trees as the fight for life ended. The cat clawed at the bank in a drenched attempt to pull itself from the creek. The animal lay in the mud as blood and life slowly drained from it.

Warm, panting breaths flowed over her body as Rosa curled by her side.

Early the next morning, Place and Salvador walked down to the end of the ranch where Salvador had volunteered to explain to him the intricacies of irrigation. As they approached the southernmost pastures, the ones nearest Miwok Creek, they talked freely, revealing more about themselves. The sound waves of their voices flew into the cool air where they landed in the auricular senses of the sleeping dog. In return, Rosa sent out a stream of dot-dashed barks. Curious, Place and Salvador jumped the fence and walked down to the creek. In the muddy bank sat the maternal Airedale with the dying cat at her paws.

"What the hell is—" Place started and then switched. "Rosa! We thought we lost you. What are you doing down here?"

Salvador knelt down to inspect his bloody and mud-caked cat. "Va a morir," he said, offering a grim diagnosis as he shook his head. He looked at the muddy bank, and noticing a spray of feathers, picked one up. "Tecolote," he whispered with an air of reverence as he held the owl's feather in front of him.

But there was life in Gatita's glassy eyes. There was a fortitude that asked for one more chance. Salvador picked up his cat, and he, Place, and Rosa walked back to the ranch house.

"Put her down here," Mitch instructed as she pointed to a folded blanket on the floor of the washroom. She had scissors and gauze in her hands, and she was as ready as an emergency room doctor. "That's a nasty tear. Her whole side is virtually ripped open. At least it's not too deep. But she has a star-shaped puncture on her other side. That one could be deeper. All we can do for right now is cut away some of that fur, and then I'll clean her up and put some peroxide on her. We'll just have to wait and see what happens."

"Why don't we just take her to a vet?" Place asked.

"Because I don't want to move her around too much," Mitch answered. "Besides, she may not make it, and just think how much it would cost. Does Salvador have the money to pay for what it would cost to fix her?"

"¿Tienes dinero para el doctor?" Place asked Salvador.

"No," he answered, and looked down at his dying cat, ashamed at not having taken better care of her.

"Tell him we'll do our best to save her," Mitch said. Then, attempting to clear the air of gloom added, "You never know, she might make it."

"How weird, huh?" Place mused at the developments of the morning. "And that damn Rosa was sitting there like she was guarding her. It was like she called us over there."

"Where is that prodigal mutt, anyway?" Mitch asked. "We're going to have to clean her up too. She's a mess. Or did she leave again?"

As the suffering cat lay on the thick blanket, Salvador, Place, and Mitch walked out to the deck where Rosa was stretched out in a leisurely way, convalescing in a swath of sunlight. Patches of fur were torn from her hide and clumps of dried mud were mortared to her legs and sides. Her eyes twitched as she fell deeper into the darkness of sleep. The two men walked back to the pastures while Mitch rolled up her sleeves and prepared to scrub the tired terrier clean.

Each day was a tentative one for the injured cat. Her eyes remained glassy and tired, at times seeming to ask for death. She ate slowly and very little, but drank gratefully from a bowl of water tipped toward her to ease the pain of movement. Daily, Mitch cleaned the gaping wounds with peroxide and then applied drawing salve to extract some of the infection. She also groomed the rest of Gatita's fragile body, gently pulling mud from her and fluffing the spade of fur that represented a tail. She took some time to slowly stroke her, scratch her head, and whisper soothing words to her. And often Gatita responded by looking up at Mitch and opening her mouth to mew a silent cry.

As the week progressed, Place and Salvador asked about Gatita each morning before they headed out to the pastures. They popped their heads into the washroom to take quick looks and tell her she was not going to die. Each morning Gatita stared with fixed eyes gazing into a vacuous future.

"What do you think?" Place asked. "You think she'll pull through?"

"She's a survivor," Mitch said, shaking her head in disbelief. "She's eating more every day. And she drinks a lot of water. I think she'll make it. But we just have to wait and see."

"Salvador thanked Rosa for saving his cat," Place said. "He says cats and dogs get along better than most pet owners think. It's people who mess up the relationship."

It was a pleasant first week for Mitch and Place on StarRidge Ranch. Salvador had offered his services for free and introduced the couple to the immediate needs of the property. He was eager in his willingness to teach and help, and Mitch and Place concluded that he was simply lonely. It had been over a month since the previous owners had fled the ranch, and Salvador had remained in his little house alone during that time. He did not bother to look for work because the harvest season had ended a few weeks earlier, and winter would soon chill the county as well as the job market. Farms and ranches would be settling into the long nights and hibernating months.

He was meticulous in his instructions. Irrigating the eighteen pastures was a synchronic art. The intent of irrigating was to release the treated sewage water more than to grow pasture. Salvador explained that the green pasture grass was not that nutritious anyway due to overgrazing and a general lack of proper management over the years. Of course, the water they constantly soaked it with didn't help, but the grass was primarily something that kept the horses preoccupied between feedings—

it was not their main source of sustenance and it kept them from chewing the fence posts.

He also told Place that the local water district maintained holding ponds which filled with, after being chemically treated, the effluent of the encroaching settlements known as housing developments that were cropping up and consuming what was once ranch and farmland. More recently, so many new homes were affecting the ponds that regular relief through irrigation was vital. After the wastewater was treated and the ponds became full, it was then circulated through its own pipelines to various ranches. The ranchers received the water for free as long as they agreed to certain stipulations. One of those stipulations was that ranchers and farmers who did not strive to be marketed as organic growers agreed to use a specific minimum amount of water each day during most of the year except some winter months. The goal was to constantly diminish the levels of treated water in the holding ponds so that the winter rains could be accommodated as well as the continual human waste that flowed through the sewer lines.

But irrigating pastures was not as Place had presumed it would be. It was not merely a matter of turning on a sprinkler as one watered a lawn. This was especially true when the main purpose was just to use up the water. Salvador explained that the hoses, which were each a hundred fifty feet long and had a sprinkler about every fifty feet, needed to be strategically placed before the water was turned on. For StarRidge Ranch, an important stipulation was that runoff from the irrigation could not, must not, run into Miwok Creek. Nor could there be any ponding left by the watering, as this attracted mosquitoes and other vermin. Irrigating the ranch required a diligent eye and a sharp mind.

Salvador and Place started in one of the bigger pastures— five-acre squares of which there were six. These pastures required three hoses each, and the method was to water one side of a pasture for a day and then pull and tug and trudge with the hoses to the other side of the pasture, and hook them up for the next day's watering. The smaller pastures used fewer hoses, but the same monotonous and moiling one-side-at-a-time method was employed. This allowed for horses in pastures to remain and graze on the unwatered side while the other was being soaked. To add to the task of hooking and unhooking hoses, there was the constant strain on the legs, as Place found out, from hopping over the six-foot fences into the adjacent pastures. It was too time-consuming to walk out of a pasture, slip through the gate, and then walk into the next pasture. Salvador pointed out that that luxury was not available. Working half-days on a ranch could reasonably mean working twelve hours.

Since it was StarRidge Ranch's commitment to use up twenty-five hundred gallons of water a day, the pastures were watered for approximately seven hours each day. On each sabbath, the effluvial rains subsided.

It took Salvador hours to teach Place about the proper placement of the irrigation hoses and to explain to him how to set the timer at the pump house. There was also a logbook at the pump house, and the figures of the meter on the pump had to be recorded daily. The water district had full privileges to check the logbook at any time on any day.

When they broke for lunch, Salvador assured Place that within a few weeks he would have the sequence of moving and setting hoses completed in two to three hours. He would show Place how to repair sprinkler heads and patch hoses as the need arose.

After lunch, Salvador showed Place that sweeping a barn did not mean literally or traditionally sweeping a barn. It was more like raking the barn, but after the cobwebbed ceiling and walls were first swept. As a neat-looking touch for the center of the barn where vehicles could drive through and horses' tack was put on, Salvador showed Place how to rake from the center of the drive-through, raking from the left and then from the right. When the job was completed, there would be uniform lines in the hard-packed ground. Hundreds of chevron-lined strokes added order and symmetry to the insides of the barns.

Place was amazed by the details with which Salvador worked. He taught and worked with Place in an exuberant manner. He had a dignity about how he approached his tasks, and to him, they were important chores. They sustained the ranch, and if the ranch were sustained, that meant livelihoods would be too. "Todos tenemos que vivir," Salvador explained. "La gente y la tierra también. Todo está unido. Y ellos que no tienen respeto por eso no van a sobrevivir." Place listened attentively to Salvador's postulations of living evenly.

On another day, Salvador suggested that it would be a good idea to prune some of the unkempt shrubs and trees. They spent the better part of one day carefully pruning the three tall pine trees, and when they had finished, Salvador remarked that they looked like three skinny teenage boys who had just had their hair cut.

The entire week they cleaned and raked and wiped and yes, they irrigated. Hoses burst, and Salvador taught Place how to patch up or splice a blown hose by attaching glue and plastic couplers to it. Sprinklers became spasmodic, and a pebble that made its way up the water line had to be removed or a spring reattached to the slapping mechanism that splash-sprayed the water onto the thick, long grass. When the hoses were fixed, Salvador waved an emphatic finger at Place, warning him that the tool kit with couplers, glue, springs, wrenches, and cutters had to be returned to its place in the hay barn. It was time-consuming to walk all the way back to the barn, Salvador pointed out, but the tool kit could not be left in a pasture for curious horses to hurt themselves on. Plus, he added, it was considerate to the other workers who found a burst hose and needed to use the kit. As long as tools were returned to their usual place, things ran more smoothly.

It was hard work, as Salvador had promised.

As he worked, Place paid attention to the cars that did not appear on Sweet Wine Road. He listened for the clangor of more progressive and civilized city life, which he did not hear and did not miss. He noticed too that when a vehicle did drive by, it was usually a slow, chugging tractor or an old truck loaded with hay or pulling a trailer with animals in it. And the drivers of these vehicles, if a person was in sight, always raised an acknowledging hand, usually a rough and worked hand. The wave alone said so much to Place.

In the silent moments of steady shoveling or symmetrical sweeping, Place found himself wondering about Salvador. How peculiar, he thought, that Salvador could look so primitive, so simple, and yet know so much. He possessed an uncanny, naturalistic wisdom with animals, and his philosophy was rooted in a common sense that expressed that it was much easier for a human to know what an animal needs than it is for an animal to tell a human what it needs. In this way, you work with and not against each other. And since many of the people that Salvador had dealt with acted only a little better than animals, it was quite relevant to apply the same approach to them too. Place was also impressed by how much Salvador knew about his own language. He had been educated in Mexico but nothing close to the level or equivalence of education Place had received. He could explain and teach with an encouraging effectiveness that kept his pupil interested, immersed, and enthusiastic.

And Salvador also wondered about Place. He appeared to deny the conventional patterns and paradigms of what it meant to attain and succeed in this country. He asked many questions, and it was important to him to do things the right way as far as the ranch chores were concerned. How strange too that this blue-eyed Mexican with such an impressive American accent could pronounce his Spanish words, once he learned them, with such authenticity and fluidity. He had no problem, eventually, rolling the first *r* or the double *r* in a word—Rápido ruedan las ruedas del ferrocarril—was the exercise Salvador had tried to drill into Place to get him to consistently trill that vibratory consonant. When that idiomatic exercise made his tongue twist, Salvador offered the ringing singing song that was taught to children and that Place picked up more quickly:

r con r cigarro
r con r barril

rápido corren los carros

cargados de azúcar pa'l ferrocarril

And Place could also slide the *n* with a tilde as smoothly as a gliding, silent hawk floated in the air.

Salvador's teaching was bringing Place back to what he felt he had lost. In a way, Salvador was Place's cultural guide, and learning to speak Spanish more fluently was a step in a southern direction. It gave Place less of a feeling of being on the cusp of two cultures, of feeling homeless in an ethnic sort of way, and of always receiving only marginal acceptance from both Americans and Mexicans. Place's identity seemed to come with an asterisk, a footnote of difference but not distinction, and as they worked, Salvador would insert other aspects that he felt would cultivate Place's assimilation. One day it was an explanation of pan mexicano, Mexican bread. He told Place about two types of Mexican bread, one called calzones, that was shaped like underpants, and another called besos or kisses. Then he recounted the joke about the woman who goes into the panadería and asks first for the underpants and then for the baker to remove them and give her two kisses. On another day, it was a song: "Mis caballos y mis perros están tristes porque ayer me vieron llorar, yo sé bien que los hombres no lloran, pero yo no me pude aguantar." With this song, Salvador taught Place that animals know how their owners feel. They know when their owners are sad or mad or happy. "¿Y cómo saben, Plácido?" he asked Place and without waiting for his response, answered convicingly and with mysterious awe, "Sí, saben. ¡Es una cosa muy extraña!"

At the end of the week, Mitch and Place invited Salvador over for dinner. He ate ravenously and commented on the satisfying meal of meatloaf, mashed potatoes, gravy, cooked carrots, and warm dinner rolls. He had never had such a tasty meal. Place reminded him that perhaps he had never had such a gabacho meal, and Salvador agreed.

After dinner, the three of them went out to the deck and sat at an old picnic table where they ate fruit and cheese and talked.

RICK RIVERA

Mitch talked, Place listened, and Salvador stared. When a convenient break occurred in the conversation, Place interpreted in stalling and stammering Spanish the more important points and caught Salvador up to the discussion.

"Jacqueline and Mickey will be here early tomorrow. They're only staying the weekend, but she said there's a lot of stuff they want to get done while they're here."

Place interpreted, and Salvador commented that the ranch certainly looked better than it had just a week ago. Jacqueline and Mickey would appreciate the quick improvement. He added that he would stay out of the way, as he sensed that Jacqueline and Mickey did not like him. Place interpreted back to Mitch.

"Tell him I'm going to suggest to Jacqueline and Mickey that they keep him on for awhile. I'm going to tell her that he had a lot to do with the improvement of the place this week. He's just too valuable to cut loose right away. They should realize that."

Place interpreted, and Salvador was grateful.

That night, as Mitch and Place settled into bed, they heard the Kittles' pickup slowly drive onto the property.

"It's them!" Mitch said in a spooky voice.

"Hurry, get under the covers!" Place whispered. "You're always safe under the covers." They laughed and tickled each other and squiggled under the covers like kids at a slumber party. Then they listened for sounds that would provide clues to what Jacqueline and Mickey might be up to.

Place fell asleep quickly. As she entered the subconscious fringes of her own sleep, Mitch could hear the faint bawling of calves in the distance. Sleepily she figured that some young ones at Sweet Milk Dairy had lost their mothers.

At eight the next morning, Jacqueline Kittle strode from the antiquated milk barn up to the ranch house. She knocked loudly on the back door, setting off an alarmed ranch dog in the form of Rosa. Mitch answered the door, and Jacqueline apologized for her abruptness.

"Hi. I didn't think you'd be up yet," she explained. "But we gotta get going early around here."

"Oh, no problem, Jacqueline," Mitch answered as she walked out to the deck. "We've been up since five. Place starts working at six. We figured you'd be up here sooner."

"Well, I would've been," she began, and she did not offer the expected reason, cutting her statement down to an unexplained clause. "So how did it go this week? Do you two think you'll be able to handle it?"

"Oh, I think so," Mitch answered. "This has been an interesting week. We've really learned a lot about what needs to be done around here. Salvador was especially helpful. He worked all week with Place. They got a lot done, didn't they?"

"Hmmm. Yeah, I guess," Jacqueline responded. She was preoccupied with some of what she had just heard, and then said, "He better not expect to be getting paid. I didn't agree to give him anything. In fact I want him out of here as soon as—"

"Who, Place?" Mitch asked, knowing just when to interrupt and that Jacqueline was really talking about Salvador. She was finding her peaceful morning unnecessarily and irrationally inflicted with Jacqueline's scowling demeanor and attempted to return some of that nettlesome feeling.

"No! I'm talking about Salvador. He better not expect—"

Mitch interrupted again by clearing her throat assertively. She looked at Jacqueline with piercing eyes. Jacqueline stared back, but her eyes were not as pointed. Mitch let a few seconds of silence preface what she wanted to say, and then she began: "Jacqueline, nobody's asking you to pay them for anything. Please don't worry. Salvador's not going to ask you for a cent. But I think you should seriously consider keeping him on for a while. He knows this ranch better than any of us. He's a good worker. And you wouldn't have to pay him much. This place could use the extra help, especially now. I can do some, but a lot of my time is going to be spent getting this house into shape."

Jacqueline was not accustomed to straightforward talk. She was hoping to warm to Mitch this weekend, but there was something about her self-assurance that irritated Jacqueline.

Mitch was irritated too, and it was Jacqueline more than Mickey that created that irritation. Mitch searched for the causes and effects that directed her perception of Jacqueline and she cued them up to form her reasoning: "It's Jacqueline's money, her means that got them this ranch. Since the ranch is hers, she gets to call the shots. It's Jacqueline's ignorance that guides the shots she calls. Therefore, the shots she calls are stupid ones. It's Jacqueline's stupid ideas that keep things inert, but she wouldn't recognize progress if it walked up to her and stepped on those clean, fancy boots of hers." This much Mitch understood, and as she understood it she liked it even less. Jacqueline was coarse, another cause, and she was really deep down—but not too deep to be hidden—trash, a blatant effect. Add her ignorance and insolence to that and almost any reasonable thinker could see she was easy to classify, starting with order and going down through family, genus, and species. Mitch knew that Jacqueline held the reins and Mitch was simply another saddled beast in her eyes. This startling realization led Mitch to shudder momentarily, jarring her ego. At least with Place, they both agreed, even if it was a tacit understanding, that Mitch knew how things should progress and that she would guide Place through those things. He understood the nature of cause and effect and acknowledged that that was how things should work. It eased his burden. It allowed him to float along in a world that confused him and was one he often regretted living in. Mitch waited for Jacqueline to respond, and as she waited she recalled some lines from *Othello:* "It is the cause, it is the cause, my soul. Let me not name it to you, you chaste stars! It is the cause."

"I'm sorry, Mitch," she said, switching her tone as she confronted the fork in the discursive road. "Buying this place has been stressful for me. Everything happened so fast. I'm feeling such pressure from thinking about making the payments and all the money I have to put into this place just to get a respectable boarding operation up and running. I bought this ranch for Mickey because he wanted to get out of the construction business, and he wants to ride horses and rope. And I'd like to do that too. But it's costing so much."

"Jacqueline," Mitch said "I really think we can help you. There's a lot of work to do around here, but it can get done, as Salvador and Place say, 'poco a poco,' which means that little by little things will start looking better. Maybe I can get some horses onto this property. I can probably have them within a month. You'll have some income from that starting sooner than you thought you would. But really, Jacqueline, this ranch needs to be fixed up first. And your pocketbook can't afford to lose a hand like Salvador. Just think about it. Come on, I'll show you what we've worked on this week."

Mitch showed Jacqueline the inside of the ranch house first. She was tearing down old wallpaper and preparing the walls for painting as Jacqueline had asked. The old doors would be sanded and revarnished next. The enormous job of refurbishing the floors would take time as the old carpet needed to be ripped out and the worn linoleum had to be peeled from the kitchen and bathrooms. Jacqueline and Mitch then walked out toward the pastures and barns. Mitch made pointing motions to the left and right, showing her where they had cleaned, pruned, or moved something.

From his kitchen window, which was blocked by his outhouse, Salvador leaned over the sink and stretched his neck at an angle. With a sliver of a view, he watched the two women as they walked around the ranch. In the milk barn, Mickey stretched, scratched an armpit, wiggled his toes, wiped his eyes of sleep, and decided to wake up.

Jacqueline was not satisfied with the slow progress, but she did feel better. Mitch knew of the importance of evidence, and she made it a point to walk Jacqueline all the way to the end of the property and then over to the western portion of the ranch. It was a long walk, and most of the way Jacqueline stopped frequently to catch her breath or rest her legs, pretending to inspect a gate or check to see that a waterer had been cleaned. Mitch emphasized what was occurring with the irrigation and explained to Jacqueline the finer points of what her contract with the water district called for. She showed Jacqueline the cleaner barns and pointed out the neatly shaped shrubs and trees as well as the lawns surrounding the ranch house that were already showing deeper shades of green despite the late season.

Returning to the milk barn, they met Mickey, who greeted Mitch and expressed a distinct pleasure with the progress in such a short time.

Jacqueline remained unconcerned as Mickey complimented Mitch. "You guys really did some work around here. I can see a big difference already. It looks great. Well, we better tend to those cows."

"What cows?" Mitch asked.

Behind the barn was a stock trailer with six calves. Mickey had purchased them on the way to the ranch, and they would be the first pasture tenants. Jacqueline's and Mickey's horses would come up next week.

"What do you plan to do with them?" Mitch asked.

"Raise them for beef," Mickey answered. "If you want to live like country folks, you do what you can to raise your own food."

Mitch did not like the idea of cows on the ranch, but since it was not her property, she was not going to point out to Jacqueline and Mickey that the fencing on this ranch was suited primarily for horses. With their tendency to push and lean and want their sides scratched, cows would do a considerable amount of damage to the wood and hogwire fences of StarRidge Ranch. The fence would be bowed in no time. Perhaps the Kittles thought that since there was an old milk barn on the property, the ranch could accommodate cows. Mitch had wondered too about a milk barn on what was previously a thoroughbred setup. When she went to the title company and county recorder's office to research the history of StarRidge Ranch, she discovered that decades ago it had been a dairy, and the only remaining artifact to indicate that was the bonnet-roofed milk barn; the rest of the ranch had long since been redesigned for horses. She found out too that the little round house that Salvador lived in was what the county referred to as a "non-permitted dwelling" marked as uninhabitable due to new sewage regulations. Like Salvador, the help house was illegal.

"Where do you plan on putting them?" Mitch asked.

"I was going to put them in one of the smaller pastures," Mickey answered. "They don't need too much space for right now. The guy I bought them from said that we should probably give them all a bolus too. You know what that is?"

Mitch thought for a few moments before answering. She was starting to regret that she had lied about Manfredi's letter of recommendation and the other two mendacious documents. Once a lie was produced in one place, it could come back in a different form in another. And it became harder to justify and convince while still sorting through the dirty laundry of falsehoods that often mixed with delicate garments of truth. Jacqueline and Mickey apparently had not read Mitch's portion of the resume, Mitch thought, that said she had managed a dairy operation in Colorado. Maybe they forgot, she guessed. And then she told Mickey and Jacqueline all about what a bolus was.

"Now, that depends. Basically a bolus is just a big pill. But there are different types of boluses. Are you giving them a bolus for scours or deworming or what? Do you have a balling gun? Also, with all due respect, I suggest that you might consider putting your calves in one of the larger pastures, preferably one that has a holding pen contiguous to it. That way you can bolus each calf individually, unloading it from the trailer to the holding pen and then setting it loose in the pasture."

Mitch caught herself and realized from the day of the interview that Jacqueline and Mickey did not like her omniscient answers and advice. She added carefully, "I realize you folks are primarily horse people. I do know a little about cattle. I can help if you want."

Jacqueline declined as an impressed Mickey accepted Mitch's offer.

"Let me drive down to one of the pastures to get things in position," Mickey said, his voice rich with excitement. "Jacqueline, would you fetch my rope?"

The six calves were unloaded into a large pasture. Mickey drove the pickup with the stock trailer hitched to it out of the way, and he, Jacqueline, and Mitch watched as the calves inspected their new arrangement. These were Holstein heifers, dairy stock, and probably culls, as most dairies wouldn't let go of a good potential milker. Mitch wondered why Mickey would purchase these calves for beef rather than the more desirable and better meat-producing, black-bodied and white-faced or Angus bull calf. But Mitch was also starting to grow accustomed to the pattern of ranch business the way the Kittles conducted it.

Mickey swung his rope over his head a few times and aimed the lasso at a fence post. After missing repeatedly, he declared he was ready. Mitch was concerned that the cattle had been released from the trailer into the open pasture all at once instead of situating the trailer close to one of the holding pens and cutting one calf out at a time, as she assumed would be done. She was interested to see how Mickey's method would work. Perhaps there was a new way of administering medication, she thought, as she realized that she had not worked with cattle for over fifteen years.

Mickey instructed Jacqueline and Mitch to help him track down one of the now free-ranging calves. Once they were close enough, he would lasso the animal and they could drag it to the holding pen where they could restrain it and stuff a bolus down its throat.

They stalked the first randomly chosen creature all the way to the far end of the pasture until it was cornered. On the way, the calf periodically stopped, ate some grass, and would lope away a little until it felt safe from its pursuers. Then it ran into a corner and would have to burst through a phalanx made up of Jacqueline yelling "yaa! yaa!", Mitch approaching cautiously and murmuring, "So, boss, it's okay, boss," and Mickey swinging his loaded lariat high over his head.

He shot the noose at the calf's head and missed. It ran to another corner of the pasture. They tramped over to where the calf was eating, suspiciously now, and again Mickey readied his loop. Mitch signaled to Jacqueline to close ranks on her side, and when she did, Mickey hurled the lasso again. This time he grazed the calf's head. He gathered up his rope quickly before the young animal could run to another corner. He made his loop even bigger, and running up to the calf, he mugged it by swinging the opening of the lasso over its head. Mickey grabbed the end of his rope and pulled hard. The calf choked out a grunt before lunging forward in a panic. Mitch jumped close to the calf and holding it in a headlock, tried to ease its fear with low, susurrous sounds. Mickey continued to pull back on the rope as if the animal had been sentenced to hang.

"Where's the bolus?" Mitch managed to ask as she continued her tight grip. "You might just try it here. This baby weighs about three hundred pounds, and I don't think it will let us drag it all the way to the holding pen. But first cut some slack or nothing will go down its throat with your rope pulled so tight."

"I have it—right—here," Mickey sputtered as he reached into his pocket with his free hand and tried to approach the front of the calf at the same time.

Jacqueline, seeing the impending struggle, scrambled up on the fence.

"Okay, hold on to him, Mitch," Mickey said. "I'm going to stuff it in his mouth."

The calf, however, did not feel that Mickey's plan was really conducive to its own well-being. As he swung his hand up to the creature's mouth, it switched ends on him quickly so that now he aimed for the part that was called rump roast once the cow had been butchered. Mitch maintained a fierce headlock on the calf as she dug her heels into the ground, and the bovine switched and bucked and jerked. Mickey's legs were scissor-locked around one of the calf's front legs now as he held onto the noose with one hand and aimed with his fist at the beast's mouth. But the animal had much more self-esteem than anyone had realized. It stepped sideways and bumped Mickey into the fence, then switched again. In the dervish of motion, the rope continued to wrap around both the young cow's body and

Mickey's. Mitch finally let go and cleared from the excited turmoil as Mickey rode the side of the calf while tethered to its body like Ahab to Moby Dick.

Mickey finally broke loose, and in a striking roundhouse punched the bolus into the calf's mouth. The shocked animal ran to the middle of the pasture with the rope still around its neck. It mouthed and gummed the large pill for a few seconds, then spit it out. Mickey wiped dirt and manure off himself and shook his head quickly to regain his senses.

"A successful ride is eight seconds!" Mitch joked. "You almost had it, cowboy."

Mickey smirked, and Jacqueline praised him. "You did fine, honey. At least you got the pill in its mouth."

"Yeah but she spit it out too," Mitch said pointing to the victorious calf. "That one's been wasted. That's why you need a balling gun. You get that bolus right down their throats with one of those." Mitch did not wait to hear Jacqueline's or Mickey's response. She walked away realizing that what she had learned years ago with cattle still held true.

"Where are you going?" Jacqueline called after her.

"I have a ranch to run!" Mitch yelled without looking back and holding her arms outstretched as a way of presenting the vastness of the ranch to the owners.

Mickey determined that he would just seed the pasture with many boluses—two for each calf—and he rationalized that eventually they would walk over to one and eat it when they felt a worm coming on or had a touch of diarrhea. He didn't remember what type of boluses the man gave him when he purchased the calves.

The weekend did not end soon enough for Mitch. Place had managed to stay busy with his regular chores and the ones that Jacqueline added later that Saturday—like washing and waxing their truck, cleaning out the stock trailer, and helping Mickey put up a large, colorful wooden sign at the entrance to the ranch that read: **STARRIDGE RANCH** in loud letters, and 1755 SWEET WINE ROAD in smaller letters. Mitch was also quite valuable by making dinner reservations for the country couple and finding out what the operating hours were in a nearby winery's tasting rooms.

That evening, when Jacqueline and Mickey left for dinner, Mitch and Place walked out to the pasture and, leaning against the gate, they wondered how they could get the rope off the persevering calf.

In a dark corner of the stall barn, two thick and calloused hands dug deep into a sack of alfalfa molasses left by the owners of Thundering Thoroughbreds Ranch. Salvador reached into the middle of the sack feeling for the sweet feed that would be more moist than the crusty and dry edges of stale feed that filled up the rest of the sack. With two full buckets, he walked out to where Mitch and Place pondered the noosed calf. Salvador slipped between the horizontal rails of the gate and spread the feed out on the ground. He grabbed at his Adam's apple and with a loud, convincing, and vibrating bellow, mooed for the calves. The ruminating animals looked up, and slowly they approached him as he continued to moo. Salvador watched the calves examine the feed and eat for a few minutes, and then calmly he slid over to the roped calf, patted its head, and removed the noose.

"Now that's a ranch hand!" Mitch glowed as she looked at Salvador admiringly. "Gracias," she said to him, bowing her head slightly in a show of respect. She looked at Place and said, "Tell him we aren't going to tell Jacqueline and Mickey how the rope came off. Let them figure it out for themselves. We'll leave it hanging on the gate. I wouldn't be surprised if they didn't notice, anyway."

They walked up to the ranch house and sat on the deck talking and drinking beer until they heard Jacqueline and Mickey's truck drive up. Quickly, Salvador sneaked back to his small home, and Mitch and Place went inside, not turning on any lights, deciding they had had enough for the day.

Early Sunday morning, Mitch and Place left the ranch to eat breakfast and talk without the interruptions Mitch anticipated.

"You know, honey," Mitch began, "I knew from the start that Jacqueline and Mickey didn't know too much, but I just didn't realize they were close to terminally ignorant. It's weird because they have all the right stuff in terms of clothes and boots and that fancy cowboy's Cadillac they drive around in. But as far as any animal savvy or basic ranch know-how, those two could be classified as remedial or even preliterate. They know just enough to be dangerous."

"When you have money it doesn't matter," a cynical Place commented. "Too bad ignorance isn't against the law."

"Well, it will matter. They need to get with it. I can't see those two coming onto this ranch and running a boarding facility. You know, I never did find out what kind of trainer she was. And it's funny, she hasn't mentioned a thing about it, either. Then they brought those calves up and plan on making them live on just the pasture. Those young ones need other feed. But I didn't tell them that. I'm just going to buy my own. You know what happened last night after I finished making my final rounds? Jacqueline told me that she and Mickey weren't quite satisfied with our progress."

"What?" Place asked as he suddenly stopped chewing his food. His face grew a darker shade as the anger filled his cheeks and shot through his eyes.

"You were already in the house," Mitch explained. "Jacqueline and I had talked about the ranch work earlier, and I thought I had pointed out what she needed to realize. But last night as I was coming in, she ambushed me and wanted to talk. So she, Mickey, and I sat out on the deck, and I gave them our side of the story."

"What do you mean 'our side of the story?' " an increasingly angry Place asked. "We don't have a side of a story because we don't need one. A side of the story implies that we need to offer excuses or something like that. Let's just get the hell out of this whole thing! I promise I'll find work someplace."

"Now wait, honey," Mitch urged. "I did talk to them, and they seemed to understand. I told them you're putting in some long days with only one break. I suggested that maybe they hire Salvador. And I did tell them to give us our walking papers if they're dissatisfied. Nobody has to get mad about anything. Look, they'll be up next week. We'll see what they're like then. You just keep working."

Mitch stopped speaking as she looked at Place and he looked down at his plate, his tired face resting on a fist as his elbow pointed into the table. She dipped her head and pushed it forward, thinking it would give her a better look at what was running through Place's mind.

She began again in a cautious tone. "Honey, look, I'm thinking they'll stay away for awhile. You know, it's kind of like when a kid sees a toy he has to have and then once he gets it, it doesn't quite fire his rocket like he thought it would. Well, this ranch is like a toy they bought. Everything's new to them. Jacqueline even asked me what the strong smell was when I was walking her around the ranch. I just pointed to the dairy across the pastures without saying anything. Ranches do have smells. And I think that Mickey grew up watching too much *Rawhide* or something. Let's just ride it out, honey. When our year's up, I'll go back to lawyering. I decided that last night."

Place ate quietly. He could feel a growing despondency flow through his mind. Indignant, raging thoughts coursed through his brain. Violent images flashed before him. "Can we go out to the coast after breakfast?" he asked. "I need to clear my head."

Mitch drove north on a desolate country road before heading toward the coast. "We belong there," she said as Place looked out at the land. As they approached the coast, Mitch looked for a special turnout, one that would accommodate only their vehicle and them. The couple leaned against the truck holding hands and looked out to where the water met the sky. Together they listened to the whip of the wind converse with the wash of the waves.

Mitch and Place returned to StarRidge Ranch in the late afternoon. They had hoped that Jacqueline and Mickey would be gone or close to leaving when they arrived.

As they drove onto the property, Jacqueline was standing in front of the little house gesturing to Salvador, who nodded his head understandingly.

"What do you suppose she's talking to him about?" Mitch asked.

"She's probably reminding him about when he has to leave," Place responded.

Mitch and Place waved to the two as they drove by. Salvador waved back, and Jacqueline continued with her hand signs and did not acknowledge her new ranch managers.

As they walked into the house, Place commented sardonically, "I think she's telling him to take the next pitch and then bunt."

Moments later Jacqueline's forceful knock resonated through the large and mostly empty ranch house. When Mitch answered the door, a proud Jacqueline informed her that she had made it clear to Salvador that he would receive no money for his help. Mitch stared hard at Jacqueline. She thought to herself that she would not even tell Place about this part of the discussion and would probably filter much of what Jacqueline had to say to her before she apprised Place of any new developments. Jacqueline was quite pleased with her assertiveness, and she informed Mitch that she was starting to get the place in shape.

"You know, Mitch, sometimes you have to kick some butt to get people to understand what you're all about," Jacqueline said.

"You sure do," Mitch responded, "especially if they need it." She imagined what it would be like if Jacqueline could kick herself in the rear with the point of her own flashy boot. The more Mitch stared at Jacqueline, the more she noticed a glazed look in her eyes. She noticed too that Jacqueline wavered a little as she spoke, and the sour scent of wine floated from her breath.

Jacqueline handed Mitch five pages of scrawled instructions and before departing, expressed that she hoped to see more progress by the end of the next week. Mitch watched as the showy truck paraded off the ranch, and slowly she read Jacqueline's instructions:

Mitch and Place:

As you realize I am not quite pleased with how things are turning out on this ranch. I am not sure what you have been doing all week but I expect an expected improvement. I want you to do the following chores this week.

1. Paint the fence. I left ten five-gallon buckets of white paint in the milk barn. Don't start the sheds yet I want to see how you do on the fence first.

2. Clean out the milk barn. Both floors. Mickey and me will be conversing the milk barn into our penhouse. We think we can move up here sooner than we thought we could.

3. Figure out a way to cut down the pine trees. Mickey hates pine trees. And save the wood. Chop it up for fire wood. We are going to put a wood burning stove in the new place.

4. Order some stationary and envelops with are letterhead. Look at the sample stapled to these instructions.

Mitch thought about how tactful she would have to be with Place when she informed him of the list of chores. She continued reading the rest of the pages, which contained largely a verbose thesis on the troubles and turmoil of owning a ranch and how "other people seem to have a hard time understanding ranch life." As the stars began to pop into the dusky evening sky, Mitch also thought that she and Place would leave StarRidge Ranch much sooner than they had anticipated. As she turned from the railing of the deck to go inside, she noticed Salvador standing at one end of the deck.

"Buenas noches, Señora Moreno. ¿Qué tal?"

"Buenas noches, Salvador. How are you?" Mitch replied.

"Fine. Can I please talking to Señor Moreno?" he asked. His mouth was straight, and his eyes drooped into a lonely sadness.

"I think Plácido is asleep," Mitch said, and she held her hands together and up to the side of her face to show him sleep.

"Oh, durmiendo," he said. "Tal vez mañana I talk with him."

From the opposite end of the deck, Place emerged. "I'm not asleep," he said as he looked at Mitch and then down at the pages of instructions she held loosely. He kissed her quickly and said, "I'm going to talk to Salvador. I'll be in in awhile. Can you bring us a couple of beers, honey?"

The two men sat at the picnic table. Salvador glided his thumb along the sides of his beer can as if wiping it dry of the condensation. Place looked up at the stars, which appeared to him to be brighter in the unlit countryside. A few crickets clicked rhythmically, and the rural smells were sweetened a little by the cool night air.

"Esa vieja es una bruja," Place said, breaking the contemplative silence and commenting on Jacqueline's witchy ways.

"¿Quién, la dueña?" Salvador asked.

"Sí," Place answered. "Y no sé por qué."

"Bueno," Salvador began, "Hay mucha gente que tiene todo en el mundo pero todavía están preocupados o tristes o no más son gente mala. Y solamente Dios sabe por qué." He hesitated to allow Place a few seconds to consider his ideas on the mysteries of humans that only God could explain. Looking up at the star-dotted sky, Salvador thought about what he wanted to request of Place. He stared at his friend, and with a hushed desperation said, "Escúchame, cuate. Necesito hablar contigo de una cosa."

Place looked at Salvador and wondered what was wrong. "What happened? ¿Qué pasó?" he asked, his face and voice exhibiting expressions and tones of concern.

"Por favor, Plácido," he said, "¿Puedes ayudarme? Quiero ser legal. Quiero ser americano como tú."

The side-slashed cat's eyes gradually began to brighten. Through days of plentiful sleep, rich chunks of tuna laced with powdered vitamin C, liquid children's aspirin, and therapeutic pampering, Gatita grew stronger and stronger—so much so that Mitch and Place were convinced that she would live, and they told Salvador that he would be able to take her home soon. Her long wound had healed nicely, although the fur was distinctly more sparse where the gash had been, and there was a noticeable fault line forever embedded under her coat. The starburst puncture on the opposite side had puckered into a hairless crater. Gatita's curiosity, that nocturnal stimulant that had led her to the skulking darkness of Miwok Creek, was retuned, and she was now much more selective as she showed little desire to venture outdoors.

When Mitch determined that she was healed enough to breathe fresher air, she carefully picked Gatita up and placed her on the deck just outside the washroom which had also served as an infirmary. The cat took a couple of test whiffs, looked around, and focused familiarly on Salvador's figure as he stood at the end of the deck. She looked past him and stared for frozen moments at the far fences that bordered Miwok creek. On the lawn, some blackbirds squawked and squabbled, and Gatita hunched low as her eyes grew big and filled with a frantic dread. Salvador laughed, and she darted back inside to her thick, safe blanket.

The following days, her curiosity greatly realigned, provoked Gatita now to inspect her new surroundings in the ranch house. She walked cautiously from room to room, and in her motion each step was slow with suspicion. She carefully looked behind, inside, under, and around things. She noticed the living room windows with their cathedral-like radiance that let in inviting waves of sunlight, and she found a home-sweet-home spot of satisfaction on the sun-splashed windowsills. Whenever Mitch or Place tried to pick her up, she would scamper back to her primary spot under the washroom sink—unless of course, she was tempted with tantalizing promises of tuna. Eventually, the wary cat discovered other favorite spots—under the bed and behind the couch—and they protected her from things that haunted her memory.

Whenever Rosa sauntered by one of those spots, Gatita would reach out a paw and slap and jab at the dog's legs. Often, when Rosa reclined on the couch or in the sunshine streaming through a window, the feline found cozy company sleeping beside the terrier.

"Well, she seems to be quite at home here," Mitch said one evening as she and Place squatted and tried to coax the animal from her washroom.

"She seldom comes out from that little den you've set up for her," Place replied. "And she won't let us pick her up. That's a true sign that she's comfortable. Cats are like that, anyway. I think she should go back to Salvador's house."

Mitch agreed. "Tell him tomorrow he should set her up a spot at his house and he can start taking care of her. I want him to take her blanket too. It gives her a sense of place."

"Okay," he said, "I hope she doesn't think this is her home now. She didn't seem to recognize Salvador the other day. Or to even care."

"Well," Mitch said, "she probably still remembers that attack. Salvador thinks it was an owl that got her?"

"Yeah, he says there's a barn owl that lives in the hay barn," Place answered. "He says you can hear it screeching at night when it goes out looking for food."

"I thought I heard something like that the other night," Mitch said. "I guess they would be competing for the same prey."

Rosa and Gatita became close companions. The ranch dog that had rescued her from the clutches of a taloned beast in a murky and dank land now enjoyed the fenced and orderly range of the more domesticated outdoors. She stayed close to the ranch and seldom showed an interest in Miwok Creek. Her morning was filled with following Place out to the pastures as he readied the irrigation hoses. When Gatita eventually recuperated she restricted her activity to daytime events, and occasionally Rosa would notice the crouching and sneaky cat lurking about in one of the barns. A sporting chase became a daily ritual; a dog chore, and something that made the day seem more productive for both.

On the day that Salvador was to take his cat home, he fixed up a corner in his bedroom just as Mitch had arranged the spot under the washroom sink. He was excited about getting Gatita back. He took the beer can from the window, closed it as tightly as it would shut, and made sure that other windows were secured. When Mitch let Salvador into the washroom from the deck, Gatita was taking a long, luxurious drink of water.

The reaction from both was melodramatic.

"¡Gatita!" Salvador exclaimed, happy to see her looking better than how he had last remembered. She stared for moments with her head lowered and her body stiff. Cautiously, she shot stilettos of puncturing glowers, seeming to recognize Salvador only as an intruder. She hissed and worked a guttural shriek in her throat that sounded like a baby crying in the distance. Salvador kneeled down and slowly reached out for the cat. From behind him, Rosa gingerly lunged forward and Gatita sprang for the ceiling. Before she landed, Rosa shot under her, through the washroom, and into the greater vicinity of the home. In the sudden confusion of activity, Gatita pinballed throughout the house. Mitch and Place ran to open each door and yelled for Salvador to throw some windows open and take the screens off them.

They chased the panicked Gatita toward the opened front door, where she was met by a helpful Rosa, which turned the cat back through the house. At the entrance to the washroom, Gatita was greeted by Salvador, who jumped in front of her and bent down to snatch her from her careening. As Gatita flew down the hallway and into a bedroom, she leaped through a widely opened window, taking out the flimsy screen, and without hesitation, Rosa the ranch dog followed.

Mitch, Place, and Salvador ran to the back deck, and there they watched as the startled cat, followed by the tail-wagging dog, ran past pastures and into the stall barn. Salvador ran after them and when he arrived at the barn, he found Rosa eagerly yapping at the bottom half of a closed Dutch door. Cautiously, he stepped into the quiet stall as his eyes scanned the dark corners and silent rafters. Rosa crept in softly behind him, sniffing suspiciously at old straw.

In the cozy personalized space of Salvador's bedroom, Gatita slowly stretched, extending her claws and hooking them into her familiar pasture of blanket. She yawned widely and lazily, and nestled deeper into the nest of her wool padding for a much-needed afternoon nap.

When he woke up early Monday morning, Place could feel the stiffness and soreness in his joints and muscles. His lower back stung with rigid pain, and his legs were heavy and tight.

"I think I know what the tin man felt like in the *Wizard of Oz* when he squeaked for his oil can. My body feels rusted," Place said as he sat at the kitchen table staring into the blackness of his coffee and then looking out at the darkness of the early morning. "I should at least be able to sleep until the sun comes up," he grumbled.

"I'll give you a nice massage tonight, honey," Mitch said, sitting at the table across from him with her notes and lists of people to call and things to do scattered in front of her. "This morning I'm going to the feed store to buy a balling gun and some hay. Salvador and I can take care of those calves now that the owners are gone. But aside from that, we agreed that this week you're not going to let him help you, right?"

"Yes, dear. I am not going to let Salvador help me, right," Place answered in a robotic monotone. He sat back in his chair and stared through Mitch as the dopiness of sleep lingered in his body.

"Well, honey, it will be better that way. Next week when Roy Rogers and Dale Evans come up, they can see how much work doesn't get done with only one person doing everything. They're going to learn the hard way, or they won't learn at all. We can play their game for a little while—I'm going to get us out of here sooner than we planned. But I'm hoping some realization and rationale pop into their limited minds in the meantime."

"They're like beasts that lack discourse of reason," Place replied. "I think Hamlet said something like that."

Place walked to the pastures slowly, feeling only a little better that his time on StarRidge Ranch would end sooner than he expected. But he was disappointed too in how things were developing. In some bizarre way, he felt cheated. Lied to. He and Mitch had seen the Kittles' ad in *Barn News*, the local equestrian magazine, and it had sounded like the perfect situation. With all of Mitch's experience and Place's willingness, they had long, honest discussions of what would be required of them. The ad was a simple one, stating only:

> On-site ranch manager needed. Couple preferred. Some ranch work required. Ability to work with horses a must. Call Jacqueline and Mickey at (737) 455-0932.

Mitch and Place decided this was something they could do. They did not expect that the relationship with the Kittles would be a stressful one; that's why country life was what it was—not stressful. Place chuckled to himself as he thought that the ad should have read "Ability to work with *owners* a must." They reasoned that if they did their work, that would earn respect and a sense of satisfaction from anybody. He knew it worked that way when he was a field worker. But now, after only being on the ranch a little more than a week, Place wanted to go home. Mitch agreed, although she possessed a willingness to exhibit a little more patience; she had a little more faith left. In addition, she mounted her defense for the times that patience and faith would not carry her through with Jacqueline and Mickey.

There was the vagueness to the ad that Mitch planned to use in her next discussion with Jacqueline and Mickey should they continue to express displeasure at the amount of work that was accomplished in one week's time. Place was doing more than "some ranch work" that was required. If anything, a definition of the word "some" would have to be interpreted by both sides and an agreeable meaning must be reached. The one hundred fifty dollars a week that Mitch and Place earned came out to too low of an hourly wage for them to feel beholden to anyone. They realized that living in the old and drafty ranch house was rent free, but they still had utilities to pay. And to keep their hand strong, Mitch and Place would remind the Kittles that Place was working ten hours each day. None of the ranchers and farmers in the county worked their hired help more than ten hours a day, and many *allowed* only eight-hour work days because they did not want to burn out their good workers. Certainly this was a convincing argument. Furthermore, Mitch and Place had decided not to move all of their belongings into the ranch house, placing most of their things in storage. They lived primarily out of their bedroom and kitchen, with the living room sparsely furnished. Mitch would use this sparseness as a visual effect. Her aim was to show Jacqueline and Mickey that they had not settled in entirely, and leaving, if it was requested of them, would not take too much time.

Place smiled as he became amused at the realization that Rosa did not even follow him out to the pastures that morning. "She's tired too!" he said to himself as he walked through the stall barn.

He worked quietly as he dragged and pulled water hoses. He noticed immediately that his extra duties were mounting because a calf had stepped on a sprinkler, breaking the plastic base. Mitch had advised Place to work at a steady pace the entire week, and not to become nervous as the work piled up. But being alone in the pastures for the first time and with the sun offering little light, Place felt insecure and unsure. He recalled things he often fantasized about. He brought back the dream he had of working a much smaller ranch, but one of his own. He imagined how his own quiet place would soothe him and he thought it strange that most people, even those who could afford to, resigned themselves to living false lives, lives that weren't genuine—they were made up and guided more by what moved them in the eyes of their peers and competitors. But there was always something specious about those lives, and Place saw them as lying lives and he wanted no part of that. He no longer wanted to exist that way.

As Place finished setting the hoses in a few pastures, Salvador strode out and quickly began working alone in an alternate field. Place completed what he was doing and then walked over to talk to Salvador about the week's plans.

"Buenos días," Place started as he approached a hunched-over Salvador. "¿Qué onda?"

"Buenos días, vaquero," Salvador responded without looking up. Wondering why Place was working alone, he asked "¿Y tú, por qué no me llamaste esta mañana? ¿Quieres hacer todo solito?"

Place explained to Salvador that he and Mitch thought it would be best if Place worked alone the entire week. This would show Jacqueline and Mickey how much they needed to keep an extra hand on the ranch, and that Salvador would be the prime candidate. Besides, Place added, it wasn't fair. Salvador had already put in sixty hours of work for free.

It was an interesting strategy. Place looked at Salvador knowing that he was thinking about it. Salvador stopped working for a few seconds to scratch the back of his head and evaluate the plan. He continued with the hose he had pulled straight, working in thoughtful silence, as Place walked to the next hose. The two men jumped the fence together as they started for an adjoining pasture.

Salvador asked Place how his back felt. And before Place could answer, he sensed that Salvador already knew. His back twitched with aching spasms. His hands were wooden, his fingers swollen from the work of tugging, grasping, pushing, and holding. His arms felt taut and taxed, his biceps and forearms announcing a burning strain at even the slightest effort. His legs were cumbrous, inflexible and compacted, so that each step was really a movement in lifting his entire body as much as it was in propelling it forward. The simple act of walking became a struggle. His knees felt dry and pummeled from the pounding of repeated landings after jumping over fences. His ankles and heels flamed with sore sensations from walking in the uneven fields. And both men knew that even hot rubs and massages would do little to make oppressed muscles feel liberated. Place had learned as a child laborer that it was the mind that carried you through— if you had a strong one. Your mind convinced the rest of your body to keep at it, keep going because poco a poco, you thought you would arrive. You would start to daydream about all the things your urgent effort would earn you. You made sense of your place in the universe by convincing yourself that in the arrangement of the cosmos, your strain would eventually be eased—at least reciprocated if not rewarded. But then, after a while, even your mind could take no more, and your body refused to acknowledge what only seemed like lies.

"It's a rough life, the life of a cowboy," Salvador said in Spanish, laughing, as he seemed to mock what Place was thinking. "Y además, la vida cuesta en dólares, pero se gana en pesos."

Salvador worked with Place until lunchtime. As they ate together on the deck, Place conveyed the seriousness of the plan for him to work alone all week. It had to be done. And Salvador relented. Mitch made him feel a little better when she asked Place to ask Salvador if he would help with the calves after they were finished eating.

It was during lunch that Salvador again brought up the issue of becoming legal. He had heard of the new immigration law on the Spanish-speaking radio station. The law invited those who had worked full-time in the fields or on food- and fiber-producing farms and ranches for the past ninety days, to apply for temporary legal residency in the form of a green card. Proof of current steady employment would also be required. In exchange, those who worked and walked with the self-conscious feeling of being illegal, and lived with the burdensome necessity of always looking over a shoulder, could be granted residency for up to ten years.

Salvador did not qualify. He had worked in orchards and fields for many months when he first arrived, and even then he was paid in cash most of the time. But his most recent work had been spent on this ranch—a horse ranch—and unless Americans started eating horses in the immediate future or horseskin jackets, shoes, and belts became the fashion, his work experience would not meet the parameters of the new law, and so he did not have the necessary proof. What luck, he thought, that it was a horse that got away that day he ended up on Thundering Thoroughbreds Ranch instead of a cow from Sweet Milk Dairy. At the time it seemed like such a positive sign.

However, what might qualify Salvador, he suggested to Mitch and Place, was that he had made a wise investment a month ago as the announcements of the new law began hitting Spanish-language airwaves. He purchased the birth certificate and paycheck stubs from one Camilo Sixto Cárdenas de la Vega. These check stubs showed field work for a little more than the past ninety days, and now the newly pseudonymed Salvador Camilo Sixto Cárdenas de la Vega would only need to show documents that attested to steady, current work.

Mitch studied the check stubs and the birth certificate, asking Place questions that he then asked Salvador.

"The date on the birth certificate would make you twenty-five years old. How old are you anyway?" Mitch asked, realizing how little she knew about Salvador.

"Casi cuarenta," Salvador answered.

"How would you explain the age difference?" Mitch asked Salvador through Place.

"Voy a decir que soy alcohólico, y parece que soy más viejo que mi edad," Salvador replied, his answer oddly logical. After all, it is not unusual for alcoholics to look much older than their true age.

"Good answer," Mitch said, nodding her head after hearing the English version. "Why has the guy sold you his birth certificate and check stubs? Where is he?"

RICK RIVERA

The many-named Camilo Etc. needed to leave the country immediately, Salvador explained. It was vital to his freedom that he sneak back into Mexico after sneaking out of the county jail here. Salvador happened to be the highest bidder to the desperate man's papers, and he was willing to try to gain American residency through these documents.

"What if they think you're him?" Mitch asked.

Salvador knew that the escapee's fingerprints, mug shot, and other vital statistics were of record to local law enforcement agencies. Surely they could see that *this* Camilo was not the Camilo who had denied the secure quarters, close fellowship, and three square meals a day of county hospitality when he decided to return to his own country. Camilo the lawbreaker just happened to have the same name *and* the same birth date as Camilo the ranch hand. That happens a lot. But he didn't have the same height and weight as the Salvador Camilo. He could add that he lost his birth certificate and the fugitive Camilo found it. Who knows who *that* Camilo really was?

Mitch thought for awhile. Place knew that in her mind she was manipulating various variables. Assessing different situations. Weighing the scales of abstract justice to see how this could balance out evenly. "Let me think about this some more. I'll need to make some phone calls and visit a few people. Just sit tight for awhile."

Salvador explained that the interviews would be in three days at Grange Hall only a mile away.

In one of the holding pens, Mitch and Salvador stroked a frightened calf and assured it that the mugging it might have witnessed last week with Mickey's lasso and bolus assault would not take place here. Mitch loaded the balling gun. It was a long, thin, metal, rodlike tool with a chamber at one end which held one large pill. There was a chrome-plated ring at the other end. Salvador slowly but forcefully pressed his body against a shoulder of the tentative calf as he pushed it into a confining corner of the steel pipes that made up the holding pen. He pried the calf's mouth open a little as Mitch inserted the rod quickly and as far down the calf's throat as she could. She pushed on the ring at the end of the tool, and the bolus was sprung even farther inside the animal. She pulled the balling gun out carefully, and patted the good patient on the head before Salvador turned it back out to the pasture. Within an hour, Mitch and Salvador had all six calves medicated.

Along with the balling gun, Mitch had purchased enough hay to last a week. As she spread the feed out on the ground, she thought of the irony of fattening up Jacqueline's and Mickey's cattle, which would be slaughtered within a year. But to be food, they needed food first. Mitch was feeding the hungry calves more for their well-being than the residual effect that would produce better beef for the owners than if the calves lived on just the pasture grass alone.

In the late afternoon, as Place was repairing some of the irrigation hoses, Mitch walked out to the pastures to report her findings.

"He's right about that immigration law," she said. "It's a good opportunity for him. Invite him over for dinner tonight. We need to talk about what's going to happen."

"What do you think?" Place asked. "Do you think he can pull it off?"

"Oh, we can pull it off, all right. I'm not worried a bit. Remember, he has excellent legal representation," Mitch said, and laughed at her own comment. "My primary goal for him is to get Calamity Jane and Buffalo Bill to keep him on for awhile. At least as long as we're here. Once he gets that residency card, he'll be like one of us."

As Mitch walked to the ranch house, Place thought about how she would maneuver this challenge. Her methods and actions often made Place feel nervous and hollow, but she liked playing with the law. "It's what lawyers do," she had once told her soft husband. But during the past few years, she had begun to lose respect for her profession. She had taken numerous humiliating verbal beatings from chauvinistic judges; had witnessed in court and in chambers how some attorneys and judges were well entrenched in blatant cronyism and self-interest; and lately, she had been defeated, both professionally and ideologically, by the realization that the law differs too much with one's economic and social status. Certain individuals had better chances than others regardless of guilt or innocence. The letter of the law was an S with two vertical lines drawn through it. Place looked up at her departing figure and yelled, "Showoff!"

Mitch turned, raised a rebellious fist and yelled back, "It's for life and liberty!"

After dinner, Mitch and Place cleared the table while Salvador ran back to his house to retrieve his check stubs and birth certificate. She reviewed each check stub carefully and examined the birth certificate once more.

"Now what is going to happen is he will have an interview down at Grange Hall," Mitch began, her tone almost secretive and conspiratorial. "Interviews are all day during regular business hours and for that day only. If you don't make it that day, you have to go all the way to Sacramento. I think it's safer here. At the interviews, he'll have to get in line to get a number first. My sources tell me that there will be a lot of people out there even though many of the Mexicans are wary because they think it's a ploy to capture a whole truckload of illegals." She paused as Place relayed the information to a wide-eyed Salvador. "He's fine with the check stubs as far as meeting the time requirements. And I think now he can pull off the identity thing with the birth certificate. Tomorrow I'm taking it to an associate who can revise the dates a little. He's an expert in his field. We don't want this Camilo to have the same birth date as the real Camilo. That's just too close." Mitch hesitated and shifted the subject. "Did you know that Camilo what's-his-name is wanted for cocaine trafficking and distribution? The guy's a player, and some local authorities are very interested in finding him."

Place informed the new Camilo of the charges. Salvador did not know the particulars. He only knew the drug-dealing Camilo was in a hurry the day he auctioned off his documents at a park that only migrants and substance abusers frequented with regularity.

"Anyway, that shouldn't create a problem," Mitch continued. "There isn't even a social security number on these check stubs, which is not unusual, considering the circumstances. What he needs to do is to go to Grange Hall early in the morning. Right when they open. Tell him to talk to guys who have just had their interviews and find out what kinds of questions they're being asked. He should wait a little while before taking a number. He needs to calculate it so he has a number, but he doesn't want that number called until after lunch. Then he can get in line for an interview. But it's important that he find out what the interview is like. Who is conducting the interview, that sort of stuff. We don't want any snags or unforeseen questions to pop up. Tell him to come back to the ranch by about ten-thirty or eleven."

Salvador was impressed with Mitch's knowledge and attention to details, and he liked her approach. Up to that point, he had wondered about Mitch's take-charge attitude. He thought it odd that it was Mitch who formulated, planned, and assigned things while Place stood by peacefully receptive to his wife's, a woman's, ideas and orders. He had thought to ask Place about this, but he knew it would make him feel uncomfortable and culturally misaligned. But it was starting to make sense to Salvador, and he could see that Mitch was the strong one. Mentally and emotionally she was capable and she could face things head on, look at them with penetrating eyes, and figure out a way to deal with situations and people. The strong one, Salvador concluded, whether male or female, *should* be in charge.

He would ride his bicycle to Grange Hall early the morning of the interview and do some sleuthing. He grew excited from the anticipation and intrigue. And then he wondered how he would show current employment.

"I took care of that this afternoon too," Mitch explained. "It's nice when your friends owe you things. He'll have this letter confirming that he's employed at Paul Legarrata's cattle ranch down in the south county. It's nicely written for an old cowman."

RE: Camilo Sixto Cárdenas de la Vega

TO WHOM IT MAY CONCERN:

This will confirm that Mr. Cárdenas de la Vega has worked for the Double Oak Cattle Company from September 1988 to the present. Duties performed include caring for cows and calves, e.g. daily feeding, checking for general health conditions, maintaining pastures, and other associated work. Mr. Cárdenas de la Vega continues to be a responsible and very conscientious employee, and he is a vital member of my work crew. His application for a social security number is pending as he awaits the granting of legal residency. If you have any questions, please do not hesitate to call.

"Not bad for a Davis grad, huh?" Mitch asked after reading the letter out loud.

Salvador was pleased. Mitch and Place told him not to worry and to be prepared for the interview. Salvador asked them what they thought the chances were of his obtaining a green card. Even though Mitch and Place were not sure, they both felt good about it. Mitch's research had turned up information that showed flaws in the system. There would be a certain amount of judging going on in the interviews. Green cards were not going to be handed out purely on the presentation of objective answers and proof-yielding documents. In Mitch's experience, this created an open field of possibilities. Presence and attitude could mean as much as hard evidence. The new law was creating a mass of workers who were willing to chance coming forth to claim at once that they were paradoxically in this country illegally and wished to remain legally. There was a huge demand for their cheap, productive labor, and certainly there would be a degree of confusion at Grange Hall that day.

The morning of the interview as Salvador mounted his bicycle, Place approached him to explain a slight change in plans. Mitch and Place had agreed that riding his bike could be too time consuming for Salvador and that it could create potential snags. The plan was based on timing and strategy, and since

Salvador often paid little regard to traditional time as marked by a calendar and clock, that element was paramount and could not be tested. Another reason—an emotionally significant reason for Place—was that he would feel better if he could accompany Salvador to Grange Hall. Both men were nervous and apprehensive, and as they climbed into the pickup truck they grew sweaty and silent. Mitch advised Place, who sat in the middle, to take long, deep breaths and to tell Salvador to do the same. Outside the Hall there were dozens of men standing in front of the building. The parking lot was full, and many men leaned against cars. Others parked across the street and paced like expectant fathers. Some squatted in circles, drawing meaningless lines in the dirt and looking like kids in a huddle playing sandlot football. Place and Salvador stood off to one side by a small grove of eucalyptus trees observing the crowd and listening for bits of meaningful conversation. The Grange was still closed, but the buzz of news was that numbers would be drawn as soon as the doors opened. Salvador waited as a long line formed. He got in line behind a few familiar faces—workers whom he had seen around the county or at the park or who frequented the Boot Hill Bar where many went for overpriced drinks and paid for female companionship.

He asked many questions of some individuals who emerged from Grange Hall after their interviews. The most important discovery he made was that none of the interviewers was a native speaker of Spanish. It was turning out that communication was not as smooth as the planners and administrators had expected it to be. Those appealing for residency cards spoke a rapid-fire, staccato Spanish. Those who were interviewing and granting the cards could absorb only so much Spanish at a time. There would be many slow starts and enunciated restarts with questions and answers. Many men told Salvador that they had to help the interviewers with the questions they needed to ask. Salvador thought this could work in his favor, or, if the interviewer was not patient, it could work against him. He emerged from Grange Hall with his number and found Mitch and Place waiting for him. As they

RICK RIVERA

drove back to StarRidge Ranch, Mitch listened as Place explained, and countered each statement with a comment or piece of advice.

After further deliberation, Mitch, through Place, told Salvador to get ready for the interview. She sent Place to accompany Salvador to his small house to help him pick out something appropriate to wear. From a cardboard box, Salvador pulled out a fairly new pair of jeans—at least they were clean and not too faded, with very few holes. He also grabbed a clean T-shirt. The rest of the box contained assorted socks, briefs, T-shirts, and a hooded Sonoma State University sweatshirt. When Place asked Salvador where the rest of his clothes were, he pointed to his cardboard box. Since Salvador's house had running water only in the kitchen sink, Mitch and Place advised him to take a shower in their home.

As Salvador showered, Mitch handed Place one of his good shirts and told him to hang it in the bathroom. She took a pair of Place's dress shoes—hardly worn because Place did not dress up for many functions—wiped the dust off them, and instructed her husband to deposit them in the bathroom too.

Salvador was sweating nervously as he squeezed his wide foot into Place's dress shoes. He tucked in his shirt and combed his hair straight back. Place knocked on the bathroom door. In his concern for things to proceed smoothly, he thought about the times he was getting ready to make his first Holy Communion or confirmation or graduating from high school and his mother instructed and waited in urgent anticipation. Salvador opened the door slowly and shyly, feeling awkward in the shiny black shoes and crisp, clean shirt.

"Wow!" Place exclaimed, "¡Sua-ve-ci-to, hombre! Estás listo para ser americano," and he smiled widely.

Salvador blushed, wondering if indeed he was ready to become an American, and shifted uneasily. Mitch came to the bathroom door, seeming a bit nervous herself and trying to conceal it. She looked at Salvador and with her hands made fists with both thumbs up. "We're ready. I'm going to drive him down there. You can start on the fence so we don't fall behind in our chores. Tell him not to be nervous. He's going to do fine."

Mitch was back in minutes. She walked over to where Place was painting the long stretch of fence where it bordered Sweet Wine Road. As she approached, he could see that her face showed a concern that seemed to drain her expression of the sure confidence that he was so used to in her, and had never felt in himself. She could see in her husband the gloom he felt at the prospect of losing his new friend. Salvador was reminding Place and reteaching him the things that were culturally, genetically—essentially—his, but that he had lost through the process of assimilation in becoming more American than Mexican. Salvador had helped Place learn to speak Spanish more fluently, and he had even explained figurative meanings of what Place was considering his new language. When Place wanted to get the cracked windshield of his truck fixed, Salvador agreed it needed to be replaced because it was "estrellado." Place, asking for a clearer pronunciation of the word, learned from Salvador that the windshield was "estrellado como las estrellas en la noche," and he could see that indeed the dark night was cracked by the bright stars. Once when Salvador wanted to take a mid-morning break, he informed Place that he was only going to eat enough "para engañar a la tripa," or just enough to deceive the intestines. On another occasion when Place asked Salvador why he was often late for dinner or other social events, Salvador explained that time was not as concrete as American thinking made it appear. Salvador was on Mexican time, and dinner at six meant dinner *sometime* around six. It could be six-thirty or even seven, and that should not be a problem. Place responded that he had often heard some students in college joke that they were on Chicano time. More than anything, Salvador had reminded Place about the dignity of work, that there was something honorable about the work they were doing, even if it was often dirty and hard work. It was nothing to be embarrassed about. It was productive. And that was more than could be said about many people.

Place took long, slow, sweeping strokes of his brush, the whiteness of the paint transforming the dull, chipped fence to a glossy newness. Mitch looked over the green pastures of StarRidge Ranch and thought about the men who stood outside Grange Hall waiting for a new life. She thought about Salvador, who was the best dressed one in his odd ensemble of new shirt and shoes and worn jeans, and her thoughts turned to guilt and confusion. A significant part of why the county could boast its world-famous wines was because of the labor of men like Salvador. These ranchers and farmers wouldn't be able to stay in business if they had to do it by themselves. Most natural-born citizens wouldn't stoop to the level of work that these men did. None of these allegedly hard-working country people would profit much beyond personal subsistence if they didn't have the help of the thousands that left their homeland each year for the almighty harvest season, or to work a spread for a few bucks an hour. It was always justified by the natives as an offer of something better than where these people came from. It actually justified their exploitation. And now, to offer this promise of residency with this new law. Mitch felt that deep within the labyrinth of local and state legislation there was some dirty dealing going on. A lot of favors were being exchanged, and her reprobation led her to consider the way she conducted some of her own business. The snarl of ideas forced her to grope for allowance and forgiveness. She told herself that she was resigned, even forced, by men in a man's world to go along with this approach to be even moderately successful. But she knew too that the way wasn't always a straight one, and she thought to herself, In today's world, you can't be a crusader. You're constantly rationalizing things to yourself just so you can sleep at night.

"Your expression is a thoughtful one," Place said softly as he dipped his paintbrush in the tray of paint. "Maybe even a conscience one. Or is it conscious? I get those two words mixed up."

Mitch did not answer as she thought about how the right things were not necessarily done the right way. She felt stuck. She was bound by certain laws and regulations, but all it took was a good vocabulary and the sound and appearance of conviction in what you're arguing to switch things all around. To make things look like their opposites. To make the guilty look like victims and the victims like perpetrators. With this new immigration law, temporary legal status for one produced legal slavery for someone else. Things were so contrived because the bottom line meant so much. Profit in one place came from loss somewhere else, and it wasn't financially, either. Mitch drew concentric circles in the ground with the toe of her boot. "What's that word you were explaining to me the other day when we were talking about Salvador?"

"Parejo. It means to be honest, honorable, and on even terms with someone. That one word connotes a lot. But my understanding of the word, especially when I hear it in songs, is that there is a strong mutual respect between friends, lovers, and peers. Being parejo allows for genuine communication, even in silence. Being parejo means sincerity in relationships. Being parejo means together, like walls of resolve, you'll hold a roof of security over each other. You and I are parejo. And we're parejo with Salvador, and he with us."

For Mitch, this was a difficult concept to grasp. It was beyond her ability to believe and trust in anybody else. Frustration steeped in her mind like the percolating water of a geyser, and usually she circumvented this through fumaroles of strategic relief. But now something was different, and she wasn't sure what it was. Mitch stared at the white lines left by Place's painting strokes. Her eyes followed the fence as it ran west along Sweet Wine Road, and then she watched the road as it narrowed into the horizon past farms and ranches with postcard facades. "I'm going in to start dinner. We're going to have a big supper for Salvador tonight to celebrate."

"What if he doesn't make it?" Place asked with a crack in his voice.

"Then it will be a last supper," Mitch answered as she walked away.

Salvador walked the last right angle as he neared StarRidge Ranch. The cool late-afternoon breeze swept his hair back and made his sweating head feel a little better. For the first time he noticed how refreshing it felt. In the truck, Place pumped the gas pedal as he wondered how Salvador had done. He saw Salvador's small, distant figure grow bigger as the truck approached him. Place looked to see if he could detect an expression, either happy or sad, in Salvador's face as he pulled up to his friend. Salvador shook his head from side to side looking serious, then waved his hand in the air, holding a plastic coated card.

"¡Me dieron un green card!" he shouted as he ran up to Place.

Place sat stunned for a few seconds, and then jumped out of the pickup and hugged his friend hugely and shook his hand hard. "Let me see," he said as he reached for the card.

The residency card had Salvador's picture on it, and an expiration date that allowed him to work for five years without having to hide or lie or feel alien. The small print said it could be renewed providing the holder of the card remained an upstanding citizen. Of course, the card did grant Salvador a new name, but it was sufficient and nobody else would know.

During dinner, Mitch and Place wanted to hear the whole story. Salvador narrated that it was not a difficult interview at all. The interviewers only spoke Spanish a little better than Place, maybe, and he suggested that Place might find a job as an interviewer. Salvador's fingerprints were taken and checked, and when he had to explain the name of the criminal Camilo, things became a little tense. But really, his response and his answer to the stated age on the slightly edited birth certificate were well received. The letter of recommendation that Salvador proudly submitted, created positive head nods that showed that things looked to be in order. Most of the men who were interviewed were granted residency cards that day, Salvador explained. They had to be. There are more and more grapes being planted in this county; they need us, he told Mitch and Place.

Mitch got up from the table and took a bottle of champagne from the refrigerator. Place popped the cork and filling three glasses, they raised them in a toast to Salvador.

"A mi cuate, el señor Salvador Camilo Sixto Cárdenas de la Vega, el nuevo americano. Que te vaya bonito, amigo," Place said laughing before he emptied the contents of the glass into his mouth.

"¡No, señor!" Salvador responded, "A mis amigos, la señora Meech y el mexicano, Plácido Moreno. Gracias por todo." He stood up and bowed to his friends.

The problem with favors, Mitch thought as she drove south on Redwood Highway, was that they had the potential to create an unending cycle. It was hard to get out of granting and owing favors because one never knew when a good turn would be needed. The give-and-take of favors maintained reliable contacts, kept business relationships alive, and offered more options to situations than one would normally have. Also, favors kept the users of this system mentally sharp. To ensure that there was an equitable practice of trading, the constant evaluation of the currency of one favor against the exchange rate of another was important.

So when Paul Legarrata contacted Mitch, it was for a favor. She knew this when she answered the phone, and his voice oozed with sentiments of longtime companionship and the significance of memory. She knew too that he had most recently granted her a favor by writing a persuasive letter of recommendation for Salvador. Now he needed her to return that gesture by helping him out with something. She was caught off guard, not by needing to return a gracious act—she respected the system well enough—but by returning it within the same week. The cattleman promised her that it was not a monumental request, and Legarrata felt that now things would be even between him and Mitch. Their friendship went too far back to dispute the balance sheet of favors and to determine exactly who was even with whom, so Mitch deemed it was most prudent to stay out of possible arrears.

"Yeah, but just remember, Pauly boy, now you owe me one," Mitch said as she pointed a censuring finger at him and prepared to drive off his ranch with a timid puppy.

Paul Legarrata walked up to Mitch and resting a warm, worked hand on her arm said, "Mitchy, you know you're going to have to watch how you do business. Slow down a little and think about your career. In this county, you don't want the wrong people talking about you."

They looked at each other with knowing stares. Mitch released a silent Mona Lisa smile as Legarrata shook his head slowly. She patted the back of his hand and then gave it a firm shake before driving off and said simply, as if she were stating a fact, "You know, Pauly, I do some things in a questionable way so I won't be questioned about how I do things. That's how business and law are conducted."

It was a strange-looking little puff of fur. Most of its body was brindle in color, but there were two distinguishing markers of white: one was a goatee that blanched its lower jaw, and the other was a striped front leg. Its tail had already been docked, looking now like a grey boll of cotton. Its ears had been cut into little isosceles triangles that pointed stiffly upward from its head. Legarrata assured Mitch that she was getting a blueblood of a dog. It came papered from a lineage of intelligence and loyalty, and the reason he was giving the puppy to her was that his son had purchased the wrong breed of dog to work his cattle. Knowing Mitch's love of animals, she was the first one Legarrata called when he found out he could not return it. And really, as he explained to Mitch, this was like a gift from him to her as much as it was a favor from Mitch to him. Before she agreed to take the dog, Mitch made sure Legarrata understood that the act was a granted favor rather than a received gift. Her balance sheet would show a positive closing figure.

It would grow to be a large dog, and protective too. On the way to StarRidge Ranch, the puppy sat in a box on the front seat next to Mitch. It looked up at her with sad and confused eyes, then around at the strange space it now occupied, and howled all the way home like a lonely coyote.

"What is it?" Place asked as he watched the puppy freeze in the middle of the living room like a jackrabbit that knows it's been seen. Moments later that fear manifested in a strong stream of pee as the puppy stared back at Place.

"It's a puppy," Mitch said, patting the wet carpet with paper towels. "These are really neat dogs. I've always wanted one."

"But what kind of a furry tick is it?"

"The breed is called a Bouvier des Flandres," she said, accentuating each word just as the French would want it. "They're a working breed, originally from Belgium. They have a natural instinct for herding. They're very protective, and they like to stay close to their people."

"And so now we're its people, huh?"

"Yeah. Legarrata's son, the dense one, was supposed to buy a Queensland Heeler. But that kid doesn't pay much attention. It's a shame he'll inherit that entire cattle spread someday; he'll probably have it turned into condos—it's easier work. Legarrata doesn't want this dog, so he asked me to take it off his hands. The breeders wouldn't take it back. They're not going to give up the five hundred dollars they got for this pup. And Legarrata can afford to give these kinds of gifts."

"Five hundred dollars!" Place exclaimed. "Did the dog come with anything? Like a new car?"

"Very funny," Mitch said. "We need to think of a name for her. That's your chore. I need to think of how we'll keep Jacqueline and Mickey from finding out about her. I might just exercise some blackmail if I need to. If the puppy goes, we go."

"And what if they say fine, go?" Place asked, "Then what? Our condo is rented."

"Don't worry, honey. I've been working some things out. Making important phone calls. The rodeo king and queen will be here tonight, and we have to communicate with them tomorrow. There's no way around that. But I won't take too much of their crap. If they want me to manage this place, I can do that. But I can only do it my way."

Place knew not to ask Mitch what she had been up to during the day. He only knew that somehow she would work things out. He knew that Legarrata wasn't the only one she spoke with today. They could very well end up living someplace else by the time this weekend was over, or she could have Jacqueline and Mickey tuned in to ranch ways that would make everybody happy. The outcome could fall anywhere on the spectrum of possibilities. At times it made him uncomfortable, but he was learning that with his wife he needed to be ready for those endless possibilities that often required an open mind and quick motion.

Place lay down on the living room floor and nudged close to the puppy as he thought of what to name her. He petted her gently and talked to her cooingly. Her eyes were deeply honest ones, and they darted from looking at Place's face to looking around the hollow room, to growing bigger at the sight of Rosa. He realized it would take some time before the dog would relax and get used to its new family. Rosa had exhibited the same stiff reticence the first day they brought her home and for some days thereafter.

"What should I name you, little one?" he said as he talked to the puppy. "You're Belgian. Maybe I can give you a name that sounds European, like Jacqueline. I can call you Jackie for short. And we can say, 'People who know her call her Jackie.' Your eyes have a certain spark to them. They're reserved but trifling too. There's a hint of playfulness. I think we'll name you Coquette."

Seeing the display of emotion heaped on the newcomer, Rosa came closer, sniffed at the ball of a tail, and wedged herself between Place and the puppy. She sat in a silly and rude way as she sought the same attention by pushing her nose at Place's arm, directing it to her head or back to get the necessary loving tactile activity.

The puppy looked up at the big dog and then at Place. He informed it that they were all of the same pack.

In the milk barn, Jacqueline and Mickey lay on a rollaway bed. She snuggled close to him and pulled the blankets up and over her shoulders. They had spent a chilly and damp night in the barn, and the late October morning sun was slow to warm things up.

She nibbled on his shoulder and pulled lightly at the hairs on his chest. "Are you awake?" she asked.

"Yes," Mickey answered as he stared at the cobwebs hanging from the ceiling.

"Do you want to be really awake?" Jacqueline offered.

"Sure," Mickey responded unenthusiastically.

"Well, thanks a lot!" Jacqueline said, feeling hurt at Mickey's lack of passion.

"I'm sorry, Jacqueline. I just have a lot on my mind. I'm wondering how they did this week."

Jacqueline left little kisses on Mickey's chest as her hand rubbed its way down to his midsection. She hesitated and said, "Oh, let's worry about the slaves later. We warned them."

"Yeah, but I'm not too sure about them," Mickey said. "That Mitch seems kind of headstrong, like your donkeys. But maybe we ought to let her run things the way she wants." Mickey stopped as he thought about the boldness of his statement and wondered how it would be received. "I mean, I'm learning a lot from the roping videos, but she does know some things about managing a ranch."

Jacqueline stopped her amorous advancement. She didn't like the fact that Mickey had been thinking of Mitch. Her hand came up from his belly, and she pushed herself away from him. Sitting up, she grabbed a blouse and put it on quickly.

"What's the matter?" Mickey asked as he lifted himself up on his elbows. "What's wrong, Jacqueline?"

"Nothing," she said, and she rose to get dressed. "Come on, we have work to do." She left Mickey in semi-stiff anticipation, and swung the barn door open, letting in the cold air and the bright sun at the same time.

After visiting Salvador's outhouse where she draped layers of tissue around the opening of the rustic toilet seat to protect her sensitive skin, Jacqueline walked up to the ranch house. She held her yellow pad in one hand and shifted uneasily as she waited for someone to answer the door. From the back bedroom, Rosa and Coquette ran to the front door barking like junkyard dogs. How odd, Jacqueline thought, at the sounds of two kinds of barks. She knocked again, and not waiting for an answer, she walked around to the back door. She knocked again, and hearing only the deep barks of Rosa, she tried the door.

The Airedale sprung ferociously at the small opening and welcomed the owner with snarling teeth. Jacqueline jumped back. She licked her lips and clenched her obtrusive jaw as she looked around.

In the farthest pastures, Place knelt near a hose and painted glue around the cracked line that sprayed water wildly when he had turned the pump on. Mitch fed the calves in the pasture across the roadway from where Place worked. She wondered what surprises the Kittles would have for her this weekend, and she was glad that she and Place had Sundays off. They would leave the ranch early in the morning and stay away all day, driving out on Sweet Wine Road and then taking the coast highway north until they felt like turning around.

As Mickey dressed himself, Jacqueline told him to tell Mitch, as soon as he found her, that they needed to talk immediately. "Did you look out back?" he asked her as he pushed a foot into a boot.

"No," Jacqueline replied, "I'm not walking all the way out there. Where the hell can she be? She has no business out there."

"Why are you feeding the calves?" Mickey asked when he found Mitch leaning on the pasture gate watching the chewing cattle.

"Well hello to you too, cowboy," Mitch said as she smiled broadly. "Your rope's hanging on the gate of the corner pasture if you're wondering. How's Miss Jacqueline?"

"Oh, she's Jacqueline," Mickey answered shaking his head. "She wants to see you pronto. Like right now."

"I'm sure she does. I'm sure she has all hell to throw at me for whatever she can think up." Mitch turned and headed for the ranch house. She walked with clenched fists, and when she glanced over at Place, he blew her a kiss and offered a thumbs-up sign.

Mickey ran up to Mitch, sensing that he needed to offer an explanation. "Now, Mitch, I know things have been a little tight around here, but you need to—"

Mitch interrupted as she picked up her pace to add a degree of drama to the situation. She was surprised that Mickey was showing a trace of awareness and realization. Without looking back at Mickey she said, "Things are only tight when you folks show up!"

"Wait a minute, Mitch!" Mickey ordered, not liking how his hired help talked back. He ran to catch up to her as she entered the stall barn.

Mitch stopped and turned quickly, standing only inches from Mickey, who had to backpedal to keep from running into her. "What?" she said, shooting a bitter stare at him.

He hesitated for a moment and then began. "Mitch, we're under a lot of strain. This ranch means a lot to us, and we need to make sure things are going right. Jacqueline is really feeling the pressure because it was her money that got us in here. This is a major investment for us. To tell you the truth, we're going to have a hard time with the payments. We can do it, but it's taking everything we got. I'm just asking you to think about what we're going through."

Mitch looked at Mickey's pleading eyes. She felt a coursing anger from the narrow logic he expressed. It was a logic that demanded understanding for the owning parties while the others worked under the critical control of those who liked their proprietary position. She was willing to accept that they were all in this together and that together they would master this ranch and make up for the neglect that had deteriorated the property. She and Place were feeling the physical strain from the demanding work. They felt pressure too, but it seemed so unnecessary.

"I'm sorry, Mickey," Mitch said, softening as she bit her lower lip.

As she approached the ranch house, Mitch could see Jacqueline standing at the edge of the deck with her hands on her hips. For a fleeting moment, Mitch recalled a childhood memory of taking a horse out of its corral without her parents' permission and riding it bareback into the hills behind her house. In that recollection, it was Mitch's mom who stood on the back porch with her hands on her hips, her short-fused patience starting to burn as she waited for her bullheaded daughter.

"What happened, did Mickey catch you in the barn making out with your husband?" Jacqueline sneered.

"No. I was in the barn with your husband," Mitch shot back. "How are you, Jacqueline?"

"Fine," Jacqueline answered, feeling stung by Mitch's impudent remark. "It looks like it was another slow week, huh?"

Mitch walked over to the picnic table, and as she sat, she thought about how to handle Jacqueline Kittle. "What do you mean by slow?" she asked, maintaining the cool composure that reminded her of performing in the courtroom, and challenging Jacqueline with a straightforward look as Jacqueline looked down at her yellow pad.

Jacqueline hesitated with Mitch, which was unusual for her. Having owned a bar and having been a landlady of other properties for many years, she was used to being the one who said things—anything, and made demands, and what she said was the last word. Not many people talked back to her. She had things some people needed like jobs and homes and loan money, and those employees and tenants and friends knew better than to cross Jacqueline with insolent talk or resistant actions. Mitch didn't respond this way. She seemed not to understand the simple, implicit hierarchy of the relationship as far as Jacqueline was concerned. Jacqueline tempered her comments, or tried to, and said, "Why don't you tell me what you and Place have accomplished this week?"

Mitch was more than willing. She started with the work Place had done which, aside from the irksome hours spent repairing hoses and replacing stepped-on and stone-clogged sprinklers, included his painting the entire perimeter fence. Slowly and tediously Place had circled the ranch, painting the single top boards that ran horizontally and the vertical wooden posts that connected the boards and the hogwire. There were also the reinforcement boards at the corners of the property that had to be painted. He had started on some of the fencing at the inner locations of the ranch that formed the numerous pastures, but he got no further than that. There was a lot of fence. Mitch wanted to recite a list of things that Place had done. Mentioning only the fence being painted did not seem like much work, and she felt that Jacqueline would be more pleased, if there was such a thing, if she had listed many little jobs Place had done. She switched to her week's accomplishments and informed Jacqueline that the living room, the bedrooms, the den, and the hallways were freshly painted. All that was left for the inside walls was the wallpapering of the bathrooms and the kitchen. Along with sanding and varnishing the doors, those tasks would be completed next week.

What Mitch really wanted to point out to Jacqueline was that without Salvador's help, getting the ranch into operating business condition would proceed much more slowly. Jacqueline had no real sense of the time that certain chores and tasks took. One man working sixty acres wasn't a fair fight, and Mitch knew that Place would eventually lose the battle, no matter how hard he tried to keep up. She decided instead to avoid that approach, thinking that perhaps Jacqueline would distort the true meaning and suggest that Salvador was just another lazy Mexican. Mitch stopped with the best tangible evidence she had and waited reluctantly for Jacqueline to respond.

Jacqueline snorted, unimpressed with the progress, and said, "Are you sure I'm getting my money's worth?"

Mitch took in a long, calming breath through her nostrils and slowly exhaled through her slightly parted mouth. She ran a finger along a crack in the picnic table, thinking about why she had become a lawyer. Thinking about the injustices done to those who rarely had a voice, and now, in this setting, feeling so much like those she had tried to defend. She had thought that through her words and actions, some people would get the opportunity to explain that a human life is made up of experiences and events that tweak it one way when the rest of the world is going the other. She wondered what had happened to Jacqueline as a child, and she thought maybe something might have happened to her in previous relationships as an adult. Mitch wanted to tell Jacqueline that she understood, that things happen to people, and the hurt quite often doesn't go away. Her training had taught her that most criminals come from backgrounds of being abused in some of the most hideous ways. They strike out at society in their anger and pain because they feel that nobody cares, which for them is a reality.

"I'm not a counselor, Jacqueline," Mitch finally said, "so I won't pretend to know what's bothering you. I don't even know if you realize you are the way you are. But for hard-working, peaceful-living country folk, your attitude and timing seem to be way out of line. I'm not sure why you picked us to manage and work your ranch in the first place."

Mitch thought about her own background growing up in the country. Her father, an attorney, couldn't handle the pace of life in Los Angeles, so he moved his wife and daughter out to the country. Her mother wasn't happy there, but it was a beautiful life for Mitch and her father. As she looked out at StarRidge Ranch, Mitch remembered the little five-acre ranch and the horses she grew up on and with. When her dad wasn't helping the local farmers and ranchers with legal matters, they worked hard at keeping that five acres looking like what today would be called charming. When their work was done, they would ride into the hills, where Mitch's father would read Robbie Burns to her as their horses nibbled on grass or drank from a stream. They would watch and listen to Mother Nature go quietly about her business. She remembered too how much they had to learn when they first moved out to the country. And the neighbors helped.

"Jacqueline," Mitch said, "I want you to know that Place and I can help, but we won't be treated like chattel. If you aren't pleased with our work, just let us know. We can be out of here by the end of the day, and we'll finish the day's work before we leave." Mitch's voice was smooth, almost ironically comforting. The tone did not match some of what she said.

Jacqueline began to cry—softly at first, and then painfully and profoundly. Mitch was surprised. She had never imagined Jacqueline as someone who could cry as openly as she now did. Jacqueline grabbed her gingham scarf from her head and continued to weep deeply into it as she covered her face. Mitch reached out and slowly rubbed her shoulder and moved her strong hand to Jacqueline's neck, where she pressed with her fingers in massaging strokes.

Jacqueline's tears were the only real expression she allowed Mitch to see and hear. She was the victim, but nobody could understand that. She was the one who had to go through life with her fists clenched and her guard up. She was the one who grew up never being able to satisfy her parents or her first husband. And now with Mickey, she was always wondering if she would lose him to a much younger woman. But Jacqueline never realized how she precipitated her own experiences. She did not understand that her own feelings and experiences were made worse by conditions that no longer existed or that currently did not exist. She did not look inwardly to see if there were things about herself she should change. Hers was the unexamined life.

In a pasture, as Place worked on another burst hose, Mickey watched as he talked about his hunting trip. "Yeah, me and the boys are going to Colorado for a week. We go every year."

Place continued working. He listened to Mickey, but he did not pay close attention to what he was saying once he realized he wasn't saying anything important. He thought about how Mickey's vacuous words were like having the television on with no one really watching it.

"You like to hunt?" Mickey asked.

"I can't say that I like to or don't like to hunt because I've never hunted before," Place answered, and added, "I don't think I would like it, though. I like animals too much."

"Well, so do I," Mickey said defensively. "In fact, I like animals so much I was thinking of being a vet. But there's too much reading, and you have to go to vet school for too long. Plus, I make a lot more money than what a vet makes. But you should think about taking up hunting, especially the way we do it. We really don't hunt for more than two days, and we party the rest of the time. You see, mostly we're hunting *dear* instead of *deer*. Get it?" Mickey laughed obnoxiously with his mouth open and his tongue waving wildly to indicate an action he thought was sexual. He pumped his arms in front of him and made rapid thrusts with his hips as he snarled his upper lip and his teeth clenched down on his lower lip. He laughed sadistically as Place clamped the coupler down on the hose and checked to see that it was not set too tightly nor too loosely.

"What are you doing, anyway?" Mickey asked, as he diverted his attention.

"I'm patching a hose," Place said. "We do this at least once a day on this spread, Cowboy. You might think about learning how to do it. You'll be running this ranch all by your lonesome after we leave."

Mickey suddenly grew nervous, worried that his hunting trip might be in jeopardy, and asked, "Why? When are you leaving?"

"Oh, don't get too uptight, Hoss. We aren't leaving until you ask us to or until you're ready to move in."

"I don't know if Jacqueline has told Mitch yet, but after this weekend, she won't be up until after the new year. I'm staying here all week to remodel that milk barn. You're going to help me. Jacqueline will pick me up next weekend. We're spending a few days up in a little cabin she's owned for years in Pollack Pines, and then I'm going hunting and we won't see you for about two months. You get our ranch for two months all to yourselves. Jacqueline's going to try to bring our horses up so you and your old lady can have something to ride. You must be having fun, though just goofing off with nobody around."

Place was annoyed with Mickey. He talked too much, and much of what he said was nothing that Place cared to know about, except maybe the latest development that the Kittles wouldn't visit the ranch for two months. Listening to Mickey's prattle seemed to anger Place, and he admitted to himself that he was jealous. He was jealous of all of the things Jacqueline and Mickey owned and could do. He wondered where they got their money, especially when what they exhibited most of the time was ignorance and illogic. Between them, they had no more than a year of junior college, Jacqueline having never stepped into a college classroom, and Mickey wandering through a year of disconnected course work until he decided there was too much reading to accomplish degree-requiring goals.

*　*　*

Jacqueline's tears began to come more slowly. She whimpered now, but the emotional pain she held in was released and eased as she confided in Mitch. "I'm under so much pressure, Mitch. I'll try to be more understanding. But it's Mickey who wants to know how much work you guys have done, and he sends me out here to be the bad guy."

Mitch felt guilty at the bitterness she had held for Jacqueline. She was confused now, because Mickey seemed like the easygoing one. None of her templates that fit people into certain patterns of human behavior that would give her a better idea of what they were really like worked for her here as they had when she dealt with defendants and other attorneys.

She apologized to Jacqueline, although she knew it was not a sincere apology. It was more like a gesture, an expected ritual of communication. Something about this whole scenario, from the day of the interview, had struck Mitch as not being right with the already irrational world she had thought she was prepared for. And then Jacqueline surprised her again.

"I'm thinking of letting the Mexican stay on," she said.

Mitch wanted to jump up and cheer. She wanted to shout it from the rooftop. She wanted to tell Place and Salvador the news, and at the same time. But she sat objectively as she waited to hear more of Jacqueline's offer.

"I'm only keeping him on for a month at a time, and I can't guarantee anything. But I won't be coming back to the ranch until next year, so he at least has two months that I'm giving him. Mickey is staying here all week, and him and Place will remodel the milk barn. The Mexican can do the regular ranch chores until they finish the barn. Plus we need Place to give up his day off tomorrow. Mickey wants to start on the barn as soon as possible. Place can take next weekend off now that the Mexican will be working. We want him to start Monday. I'll pay him a hundred dollars a month and he gets to stay in his little shack. I'll be leaving you a list before I head back home. Now in a couple of weeks, there will be forty tons of hay delivered. But I don't want any of the stock fed until December first."

"Why are you having so much hay delivered when you don't have much of anything to feed yet?" Mitch asked.

"Because Mickey says the hay barn needs to be packed full. That way it looks like we have plenty of room and board for horses, and that will attract customers. Plus we did bring up three donkeys and some ducks on this trip, and next week I'm bringing up our horses for you guys."

Mitch blinked her eyes rapidly to clear her vision in an attempt to clear her mind. Donkeys and ducks, she thought. What an interesting concept. But she wondered why. And what for? Whose were they? And forty tons of hay? How extravagant. How extreme. The hay barn would not hold forty tons of hay.

"Why?" Mitch asked.

"Why what?" Jacqueline giggled at such a silly question. "They're our pets. In fact, we need to get them out of the stock trailer. But I don't want them to be given any hay until the first of December. They can eat grass until then. The ducks are going to be put in the same pen with the donkeys. I don't want too many pens to be used. The Mexican will have to rig up something over a pasture gate so the ducks don't walk under it and get away."

Mickey sauntered toward the ranch house as he swung his arms freely. "Ready to pasture the donkeys?" he called out to Jacqueline.

The couple walked toward the stock trailer. Mitch offered to help, but they informed her that they would manage nicely. Jacqueline stopped for a second and caught Mitch as she headed into the house.

"Say, Mitch, did you get another dog? I swore I heard two dogs barking when I knocked on your door."

Mitch straddled the doorway, looked down at Rosa and Coquette, who wagged their short tails, and answered, "It must have been the television. I left it on."

The three donkeys each were white with dark brown markings that ran straight along their backs and another brown stripe that crossed from shoulder to shoulder. They shuffled nervously in the trailer as Mickey backed it up to a pasture. As soon as he felt he was close enough, he stopped the truck and jumped out in a sprightly way. He opened the gate of the stock trailer and walked in. Mickey grappled with the animals as he tried to turn them out, and when one of the donkeys finally noticed the wide-open pasture he stepped out toward it. Mickey put his boot up to the animal and pushed at its rear end as he let out a harsh

"Yaaa, get out of here, Joker!" The donkey bolted. But it bolted to its immediate right and through the donkey-wide gap between the gatepost and the trailer. The other two donkeys chose the same route, and the three ran wild and free throughout the ranch.

"Mickey!" Jacqueline screamed, "They're getting away!"

Mickey watched as the three donkeys swirled around the property for a few excited minutes and then left StarRidge Ranch, running west on Sweet Wine Road.

"What are we going to do?" a shocked Jacqueline asked.

"I don't know," Mickey answered as he stood and watched the departing animals.

Mitch ran from the ranch house as if it were on fire. She hustled to her pickup and honked the horn frantically. Place looked up from the distant pasture in which he worked, and Salvador ran out of his small house holding a can of beer. In moments, Place and Salvador were listening to Mitch explain the logistics of how the donkeys would be herded back toward the ranch. Salvador and Mitch jumped into the truck and raced down Sweet Wine Road. Place was stationed at the entrance of the ranch so the donkeys would not run past him in the opposite direction. Mickey and Jacqueline walked slowly to where Place stood.

"What happened?" Place asked.

"Huh, oh, they got out," Mickey answered ingenuously.

"Yeah, I can see that," Place answered, his tone impatient. He looked at the couple curiously. Although Jacqueline seemed to be concerned, Mickey did not appear to be as alarmed compared to the urgency Mitch had shown. Maybe, Place thought, they were so alarmed that they were left mute with their mouths agape as they looked into the horizon of Sweet Wine Road.

Slowly Mitch drove the truck behind the three donkeys with both doors open to serve as shields that would discourage them from proceeding in the direction they had been when she had caught up to them. She took up the entire road as she snailed along, and hoped that no other vehicles would approach until they made it back to the ranch. Salvador walked in front of the truck waving a T-shirt like a switch. Occasionally, a fugitive donkey would look back at freedom, and Salvador would snap his T-shirt at it to keep it in line.

As they approached the ranch, Mitch yelled to Place and the ranch-owning couple to flap their arms out to their sides and direct the animals onto the property. Place flapped his arms like a fledgling, and Jacqueline waved her arms with the fluttering motion of an angel's wings while more demonstratively shouting, "Yee haa!" Mickey, who had retrieved his rope while the trio of long-eared runaways were being herded back, spun his lasso in the air and let out short, sharp whistles as if he were on a cattle drive. As the procession turned onto the ranch, Mickey tried to lasso a donkey, and when he missed, he ran up to all three closely herded animals and whipped at them furiously with his rope; the donkeys scattered to different points on the property.

"Mickey! What the hell do you think you're doing?" Mitch screamed at him, her body halfway out of the truck and her face blooming with red. "Place, close the main gates!" she ordered. "At least they're on the property. Now we just need to try to get them in a pasture."

Jacqueline ran up to Mitch and said threateningly, "Mitch, don't you ever talk to my man like—"

"Shut up, Jacqueline!" Mitch lashed back. She walked up to Mickey and grabbed at his rope.

Mickey pulled back quickly, jerking Mitch toward him, and when he did, Place and Salvador ran up to Mitch's side. They did not realize it as much as Jacqueline noticed it, but the two men had their fists clenched. Their looks and the taut silence revealed a readiness.

Mitch calmed down enough to let out a deep breath. She looked at the ground, and then at Mickey's cowboy boots—up to his unworked, creased jeans, his big silver unearned belt buckle, and then directly into his eyes. "You know what, little cowboy," she started, almost whispering, "If I ever see you whip at an animal again, I can promise you all hell will break loose. And if you want to try me now, go for it, Peter Pan."

Mickey threw his rope down and walked toward the milk barn, his boots punching solidly into the ground with each step. Jacqueline followed him dutifully as Mitch, Place, and Salvador readied to capture one donkey at a time.

When they had secured the last donkey—due to the convenience and proximity of pasture gates, each was in its own pasture now—they walked back to the ranch house. From the milk barn, they could hear Mickey yelling violently, but they were not close enough to make out all of what he was screaming. They could hear emphasized words and phrases that gave them a better indication of what might be disturbing Mickey so. "That bitch . . . !" and ". . . humiliated me. . . !" and ". . . my ranch . . . !" and ". . . you didn't even say anything. . . !" and ". . . you didn't stand by my side. . . !" and then a bitter laugh and more, ". . . try to take my rope, will she . . . !"

On the deck, Mitch stood with her father's old buck knife and cut Mickey's rope into little phallic lengths. "I'll get lunch in a minute," she said, as a frustrated tear popped from her eye.

Mitch, Place, and Salvador sat quietly as they ate. Neither wanted to break the uneasy silence, so they paid close attention to their food.

Finally, Mitch looked at Place and said, "After lunch, I'll go tell Jacqueline we'll be gone by tonight."

"You don't have to tell me," Jacqueline said as she approached the table abruptly. "And you don't have to leave. I want to apologize for what happened earlier, and Mickey and me would like to take both of you out to dinner tonight."

"Jacqueline, I'm sorry too," Mitch said. "And I appreciate your offer for dinner, but I'm just too tired. Place can go. Tell Mickey I'm sorry for blowing up out there."

At dinner that evening, the conversation was focused on Mitch's explosiveness. The Kittles pried and probed at Place, asking personal questions and making insensitive remarks. Place did not say much. He offered incomplete, vague answers. He wanted to tell the couple that they were not only crossing certain boundaries, they were virtually stomping on anything that might resemble a boundary. Did they really expect him to say derogatory things about the one person who had helped him through so much? The one person with whom he was truly parejo? They framed much of their discourse in light jokes to make their questions and comments seem more innocuous. Mickey joked that Jacqueline was his boss as Mitch was Place's, but that Place didn't seem to know how to get in good with his boss. Jacqueline added that Place must at times feel "emansculated" because of the way Mitch had to run things and Place simply did what he was told.

Place had encountered other couples like these two before—perhaps not as far out—but exhibiting some of the same clues. It was a strange dynamic, really. They would gang up on a poor, unsuspecting slob for their own self-satisfaction and degree of esteem, but alone, they were never quite as close to or fond of each other as the ganging up might have made them appear. One of Place and Mitch's favorite pastimes was revealing to each other after a social gathering what one side said about the other. How one of the partners would express unhappiness about their marriage. How the other would say he was bored with the same sexual partner. How they seemed to be at such polar opposites, and that they were now opposites that no longer attracted if they indeed ever had. Place and Mitch wondered how and why these couples stayed together, and agreed eventually that romance and finance were intercurrent elements for many people.

When Place decided he had had enough and his anger seethed through his entire body, he took a long calming drink of his beer and started with his own questions.

"Do you ever go hunting with Mickey?" he asked Jacqueline and shot a villainous look at her husband, raising his eyebrows seductively.

"No. I don't—" Jacqueline attempted before Place cut her off.

"Why not? You don't like to hunt deer, dear?" Place laughed harshly while Mickey poked at his food.

"What's wrong with you, Place?" Jacqueline asked. "We should've known better to let a Mexican drink too much firewater. They go nuts on you real quick. Maybe that's what's wrong with Mitch. It's rubbing off." Jacqueline laughed loudly and looked around to see if the other patrons had heard her. Mickey laughed uneasily and with little soul, and Place laughed at Mickey's discomfort.

As a swarthy busboy cleared their table, Place studied his face. He wondered how legal the young man was. "¿Eres legal?" he asked him abruptly. "¿Trabajas muy duro?" Place added with a taunting tone. The dark man fumbled with the plates and glasses and allowed a bashful chuckle. Place thought about his own father, a constitutional illegal. As he drank from his beer, he remembered the day he walked out of his father's home. Place would not accept his father's apology for drinking too much and causing yet another violent event in the home. His father pleaded for forgiveness, explaining that he was sick and needed help, but Place did not listen. He did not stay, and he never returned.

The next day, Place and Mickey started working on the milk barn. Place, despite his lingering anger, was impressed with Mickey's ability. He had drawn a plan of what the new milk barn/apartment would look like, and early that morning Mickey explained the blueprint. The bottom floor would contain a small living room, a kitchen, and an office. The grain chutes that ran from the top floor and down to where decades prior milk cows had stood to eat would be dismantled and removed. The upper floor would be stabilized with railroad ties that maintained a rustic look, and the upstairs would become a master bedroom complete with a tub big enough for two and a four-stool bar in one of the corners. Mickey even planned to attach a small balcony—also big enough for two—off one side of the master bedroom. From that balcony the purview of the entire ranch could be captured.

Place was also impressed with Mickey's patience in explaining how the project would unfold. Previous experience of working on construction sites had taught Place that one could only learn by being yelled at, and his disposition was too sensitive for yelling. They worked diligently, and on a couple of evenings after a long work day, Mitch and Place could hear Mickey hammering and sawing into the night.

"I wonder what happened," Place said as he and Mitch lay in bed listening to the busy hammering. "Jacqueline must have made a few things clear to the boy before she left. I didn't think he could work like that."

"Yeah, I'm surprised myself," Mitch said. "And it looks like he knows what he's doing."

"Oh, he does," Place said without hesitating. "The guy knows building. He's just kind of short with a lot of other things."

"Did he buy the story about Coquette?" Mitch asked.

"Easily," Place replied. "He didn't even flinch when I told him she was Salvador's pup and he would be taking her with him when he left next week. But now that he's staying, it's reasonable that the pup should stay with him. He agreed. I'm just wondering what Jacqueline will say when she comes back."

* * *

Salvador continued to work on the ranch with his persistent enthusiasm. He finished painting the fences and he worked devotedly on the hoses that burst with more regularity each day. He once again had a place in the world—a place on this ranch, even though he understood his position was on a monthly basis. In a sense, he had experienced two lives on the same ranch: an illegal one and a legal one.

Having a green card made Salvador a much more social being. A couple of times during the week, he visited the Boot Hill Bar and danced and drank with an ease he had never felt before. He would ride his bicycle home when his revelry was over, and he was dependable in waking up early to begin his ranch duties.

At the end of the busy work week, as the milk barn was quickly transformed into a very trendy apartment, everybody on the ranch looked forward to the weekend for various reasons.

Jacqueline drove the right angles as she approached StarRidge Ranch and thought about the next few days she and Mickey would spend in her cozy cabin. She would suggest to Mickey that maybe they could move onto the ranch after the new year as soon as the rains subsided. Together they would work the ranch as she had seen Mitch and Place do. And together they could do the things that she had daydreamed about and was imagining as she turned onto her property.

Mickey was exhausted as he walked around the new apartment applying some finishing touches. He was excited too. He looked forward to his hunting trip and thought about all the fun he had had the year before. He still had the address of a female friend, and he was anxious to see her. He even missed her, and a few times during the week he had called her to assure her that they would spend as much time together as possible. She was a wiry young cowgirl who had caught his eye one night in a bar the previous year. She had made him court her for the rest of the week before giving herself up to him the day before his hunting trip was over. This courtship impressed Mickey. It was a more romantic relationship than he felt he had with Jacqueline, who offered no challenge on their first date, and since, often blamed her lack of steaming passion on the interferences of economics and the demands of a busy schedule.

Place was looking forward to watching the Kittles' red truck drive off and knowing that they would be gone for the rest of the year and possibly longer. He knew that he, Mitch, and Salvador could work without meaningless distractions, and at least for a little while it would be as if the ranch was theirs. He was also looking forward to the new year. He felt good about knowing that they would not stay on the ranch as long as they had anticipated. It had been a good learning experience thus far, but the pressure, both physical and emotional, was disproportionate to the setting; country living had not seemed to be much different from city life.

Mitch stood in the kitchen looking out at the ranch as she peeled some carrots. Rosa and Coquette sat at supreme attention in the kitchen waiting for anything that might be offered to them or fumbled onto the floor. Mitch imagined the ranch as her own. She pictured many horses in the pastures languishing with their heads down and switching their tails casually. She dreamed about how she and Place, and Salvador too, could run a successful boarding business and seldom need to leave the ranch to earn their money. She listened to the birds as they chirped and sang and nestled in the trees to roost for the evening. She watched Gatita walk lazily from the stall barn to her home with Salvador where she knew food was more reliable. The donkeys paced in their pastures nervously, expecting to be fed just as the calves were, but were left disappointed and expressed that frustration with braying crescendos as they strained with their necks and pointed their pleading snouts upward to a negligent god. Mitch and Place had come to find the donkeys' early morning braying more effective than a rooster's crow. But the donkeys' honking had a certain quirkiness to it as it developed slowly and then screamed with operatic effort. The corralled ducks huddled in a corner like frightened immigrants, and tried to stay away from the brutish donkeys. Mitch looked at the waning sun as it shot the last of its glistening rays and illuminated the green of the pastures, and she thought about how she would make some changes as soon as Jacqueline and Mickey were out of the county.

Salvador popped a beer open as he poked at a piece of meat. He turned the flames of his camp stove, situated on the old stove, down and prepared to eat his quick supper before venturing into town. He liked Mitch and Place more than he had liked the previous owners of the ranch. They were industrious; they worked hard, and they could work long days. They showed Salvador a respect that very few people, especially Americans, had ever shown him. They never looked at him with wide eyes that spoke of fear or indicated a bizarre strangeness in the man's appearance. They spoke to him and worked with him as if they were all equal partners in the effort of living. And now that effort seemed more worthwhile. Salvador felt that he was slowly, poco a poco, moving toward what he wanted from the world. He saw himself becoming a good American. He fantasized about a job that didn't make his body ache. He imagined buying a truck and retiring his bicycle. He envisioned his own home, something modest, maybe even an apartment. He thought about how he could be happy with Gatita and he pictured in his mind the elaborate scratching post he would buy her, the kind he had seen in the window of a pet store that had cubicles with holes and platforms at different levels, situated at the ends of branchlike appendages. For Salvador, this was not too much to ask, and his effort should yield at least those simple things he limited his thinking to.

Jacqueline hoped that Mitch and Place would appreciate the fact that she hauled Mickey's and her horses up especially for their use. As they turned the horses out into a pasture, Jacqueline looked at Mitch and nodded her head proudly and tightened her jaw noticeably. It was a defiant look, and with it, she seemed to be indicating to Mitch that her country life was complete now that there were horses on StarRidge Ranch.

Mitch watched the horses, unimpressed. "That's a nice-looking little trail pony you have there," she said to Jacqueline, not really liking the looks of the animal, but trying to be as cordial as the relationship allowed. "Is that horse of yours trained for cuttin'?" she asked Mickey as he watched his horse with the pride of a parent watching an athletic son.

"Huh? Oh, yeah. You bet!" Mickey said after finally catching on to Mitch's question. "My boy's trained for roping."

Probably more than you'll ever be, Mitch thought to herself before responding out loud. "He's kind of tall for a rope horse. What's he top out at? He looks close to seventeen hands."

"Almost," Mickey replied. "He's about sixteen-five, sixteen-six."

Mitch wondered why Jacqueline had even bothered at their first meeting to mention that she was a trainer. She wondered why Jacqueline had not just said she was interested in being a trainer or that she liked horses and hoped to ride one day. Mitch didn't bother to tell Mickey that horses are not measured like inches on a ruler. After say, sixteen-three, seventeen hands followed the sequence. There was no such thing as sixteen-four or five. Mitch knew that anybody who even had a small sense of horsemanship would see that both horses were not suited for immediate riding. Jacqueline's horse had splayed and cracked hoofs, and a shoer would have a respectable project in getting

RICK RIVERA

that horse's hoofs trimmed and shod. Mickey's horse, although pumped with grace and a western flair of its own, was showing signs of not having been ridden in awhile. Besides being too fat, it ran wildly around its new pasture. Whenever it ran close to the fence where Mitch, Jacqueline, and Mickey were, it swung its head frantically at them and shied away from Mickey's hands as he reached out to pet his horse as one would pet a dog. This horse would need some ground work before anybody dared to mount it, although Mitch was interested to see if Mickey would try. It would benefit the horses immensely to be better cared for, more fit, and trained, but that would cost time and money, and Mitch's plan for this weekend was to say as little as possible. She was willing to allow that it was the Kittles' show.

Place and Salvador grappled with hoses that burst and exploded water into the air like aquatic fireworks. They too thought it would be wise not to mention to Jacqueline and Mickey that the worn hoses were needing more and more attention, and they figured that soon the irrigation period would end, offering a few months of respite. The ranch would also benefit from this. During the week that Mickey worked on the apartment, he had decided that the irrigation hoses did not need to be moved as was the custom. Salvador's labor could be put to better use helping with the new apartment. Enormous opaque ponds developed. Flowing rivulets of turgid water ran into Miwok Creek, and communities of bothersome mosquitoes were founded as the ponding created a noisome odor.

In the hay barn, Jacqueline stood with her arms akimbo and admired the empty expanse. "This will be filled with forty tons of hay by the end of next week," she said. "But remember, I don't want the stock fed until the first of December. They only have to wait about a month."

Again, Mitch did not bother to interject what her many years of ranch management and two intensive years of working toward her horsemaster's certificate had taught her. Much of the hay would mildew by the time they would be allowed to feed it to the animals. Livestock was not fed by the calendar, but by sight and need. As the winter months approached, it was vital to see to it that the calves, donkeys, horses—even the flightless ducks—had an ample coat of flesh on them to withstand the longer and colder nights.

Mickey pointed to a boxed area off to one side of the barn. It was a rectangular section with a railing built a few yards from the wall that formed a chute. He put his arm around Jacqueline, and in a fatherly tone explained, "You see that there? That's a breeding chute. You bring your horses in here and fix them up in that chute and have them go at it until they're done making a baby." Mickey was proud of his biological knowledge. Jacqueline whispered seductively into his ear, and they both giggled and pinched at each other for a few seconds.

Mitch wanted to laugh profoundly, but then she thought about the serious and dangerous implications of what Mickey had explained about the breeding chute. She was surprised that he knew what the rectangular area was, and she wondered where he had picked up that bit of information. She thought back about the day—and the way—she explained the breeding chute to Place when he puzzled over it.

"It's a breeding chute," she started, "but don't let the nomenclature fool you. What you do is, you bring the mare in and guide her into the chute. She should be in the early stages of estrus. She'll be haltered, so you're holding her while somebody else brings the stallion in beside her. He starts to nibble at her neck and withers, and the purpose is to stir the mare's hormones up; it's like foreplay. It really should be called a teasing chute. You do this for a few days until the mare shows that she's ready. The actual conception takes place in the pasture in front of God and the rest of the world. It's really interesting to watch. But you would never ever have the stallion mount the mare in the chute. It's too dangerous."

Mitch remembered too how peculiarly interested Place was in learning about the breeding chute. He tilted his head, and periodically uttered "Wow!" and "Really?" and "Isn't that something?" That day Mitch had taught Place about other animal-related incidentals and trivia. "You know, when a cow is lying down and it starts to get up, it raises its hind end first. But when a horse is lying down, it raises its front end first to get up." Place had marveled at the bovine and equine comparison and said, "Yeah, there's something about that in *Huckleberry Finn*." "That's right," Mitch had said. "And the part about when cows are eating on a hillside and they're all facing the same direction, that's what cows usually do. They can also tell you when a storm's approaching. They'll huddle around a tree and hunker down until it passes. You can learn a lot from literature—and animals." During dinner or lunch, Mitch would enlighten Place with other things she knew would fascinate him. "Did you know that a cow is not technically a cow until it has given birth? You know a dairy cow, like those up at Sweet Milk Dairy, have to have a calf first. Cows don't just give milk automatically as many people tend to think. They need a reason to give milk. Until they do have a calf, they're called heifers." And in horse terminology and lore: "A female horse can be a filly, if it's young, or a mare if it's an adult. A male horse is, if it's young, a colt. A lot of people think a colt is just a young horse and gender doesn't matter. But if you refer to a colt in ranch talk, you should be talking about a young male horse. A stallion is an adult male horse with his equipment still intact. A gelding is a male horse who's met the vet's knife and has had his mind changed from ass to grass. And did you know a horse can't vomit? That's why it's important to keep an eye on your horses. They have a sensitive internal system, mainly because of our domesticating them. But they need to be able to expel the bad stuff they might ingest, and unlike a dog, they can't just throw that bad stuff up. It can only come out of one end."

Jacqueline and Mickey brought Mitch back to the immediacy of the hay barn, and Jacqueline continued with her instructions. "When you do feed the horses and donkeys, just give them about this much." Jacqueline held her hands in front of her a few inches apart and indicated what Mitch interpreted as extreme underfeeding. As the couple and Mitch walked around the ranch, other instructions were pointed out that would involve the ranch personnel and keep them busy for the two months that the owners would be away. "And don't bother trying to put all the donkeys together. You guys put the two that go together, Gin and Tonic, in the same pasture with the ducks, so that worked out good. But keep Joker in that back pasture by himself. He deserves to be alone for leading the other two out when they ran away."

After a long Sunday of listening to more of Jacqueline and Mickey's last-minute instructions and riffling through a dozen pages listing other chores and comments, Mitch and Place stood at the entrance of the ranch and waved good-bye to the departing couple. A wave of relief rushed over them as they watched the truck grow smaller and smaller. The late October sunset was closing the curtain of human activity on another day. As they walked back to their house, Salvador emerged from his boxed home with three cans of beer, handing one each to Mitch and Place.

"¿Ya se fueron?" He asked. "¿Y para dos meses?"

"Sí," Place answered. "Qué suerte, huh?"

Salvador looked into the distant angles of Sweet Wine Road, watching the tiny starlike orange cab lights of the truck twinkling as it moved north and then east. He took a draining drink from his beer and said as if to affirm their collective luck, "Sí, qué suerte. Gracias a Dios."

And it was a Dios that Mitch, Place, and Salvador gave thanks, each in his or her own way. As November approached, the Indian summer offered a warm, temperate climate for the ranch work that remained before the rains limited the scope of outside activity.

Place watched with amazement as the forty tons of hay were unloaded from the two-trailered truck and stacked neatly in the hay barn with a forklift suited specifically to grab and move many bales of hay at one time. The barn stood stuffed with hay, and the last few tons remained on the truck.

"Well, where are you going to want the rest of this?" The forklift driver asked as he sat looking down at Place. "You have almost ten ton here yet."

"Just offload it right outside the entrance to the barn here," Mitch pointed, answering the question that was not directed at her. "We'll have to shift some things around to make room for it."

"You have about as much hay as I deliver to the fairgrounds when the county fair is in town," the driver said. "The only thing is, I don't see too many hay-eating animals around this spread. You all must be extreme vegetarians!"

Mitch shrugged her shoulders at the driver, not offering an explanation and looking, as Place and Salvador did, at the hay stacked high in the barn. There was a space from the top of the towering hay to the roof of the barn that could accommodate individual bales, but getting those extra bales up to the top would be difficult. Salvador, reading Mitch's face, explained to Place that with a ladder and teamwork, they could squeeze the remaining hay all the way to the rafters of the barn.

Place interpreted to Mitch and added his own observations in the process. "Why can't we just put the rest of these bales in the stall barn? There aren't any animals in there, anyway."

"Because," Mitch responded, "Jacqueline gave specific orders not to put any hay in that barn. She has other plans for that space. Plus, I don't trust them. They could show up any day just to check on us."

Salvador leaned the tall ladder against the piled hay. He tested the ladder for stability and told Place to climb to the top of the amassed hay. He handed two hay hooks to Place before he ascended and by the time Place was situated high under the roof of the barn, Salvador was slowly making his way up the ladder with a bale perched on his shoulder. He stood sideways on the ladder as he balanced the awkward bale and took careful, calculated steps, leaning his body as close to the ladder as physics allowed.

Mitch watched worrisomely as she clutched the ladder and looked up. Hay dust floated slowly down toward her and she visored her eyes with a hand as she wondered about the possibility of spontaneous combustion once the barn was bloated with every morseled bale. Place craned his neck downward as he held the top of the ladder.

"Be careful," Mitch offered.

"I think that's a given," Place retorted, and then said to Salvador, "Yeah, cuidado."

"Yes, mexicanito, voy con cuidado," Salvador grunted as he approached the top rungs of the ladder. When he neared the top, Place sunk the hay hooks into the bale and pulled it up toward him. As he stood at the top of the ladder with his head and shoulders poking up over the immense pile, Salvador pointed to the farthest corner of the stacked hay and told Place to begin there with each bale until the back rows were filled in, gradually working his way closer to the edge. They planned to place half of the excess hay up to the rafters on the one side of the barn, then switching to the other side to fill in that stack.

"If we still have some bales left over," Mitch said, "we're just going to fill in the aisle. That's the best we can do. And when we feed, we'll take from there first, then pare down these stacks as soon as we can."

Mitch dragged the bales of hay to the bottom of the ladder where Salvador would lump one onto his shoulder and start the long, slow climb. Place knelt at the top with hooks in each hand, ready to relieve Salvador of the bale as soon as he was close enough.

They worked steadily and quietly for most of the day. The only sounds that echoed through the hay barn were the swishing drag of the bales that Mitch pulled toward the ladder, the accomplished grunts of Salvador heaving a bale on his shoulders, and the crunching jabs of Place's hay hooks stabbing into the bale.

"Somos como hormigas," Salvador said as one side of the hay barn grew plump with the bales that were locked into the last spaces like a completed puzzle.

"He said we're like ants," Place informed Mitch as they stood in the middle of the hay barn and assessed the remaining side to be filled in.

Salvador continued with his analogy, explaining that ants were a lot smarter in the way they worked than what the trio was presently experiencing. Ants, Salvador said as he looked at both Mitch and Place while catching his breath, work in the opposite way that we do. When they dig out their ant holes, they take each grain a measured distance away and gradually work closer and closer to their entrance. So the more they work, the shorter the distance they have to go with each grain of dirt. But we started out carrying our grains of baled hay farther than we should, and we'll end up carrying them just as far when we finish. We don't get that much of a break with dragging, lifting, and squeezing these bales into the rafters. Too bad we aren't as smart as ants he concluded as he motioned for Place to climb up to his hooking position.

Place hooked and lifted the last bale of hay, and with the precarious, limited space, he pushed the bale tight against the others. He looked at Salvador for approval, who looked past Place wide-eyed and silent. Place slowly looked over his shoulder, and in the deepest corner of the packed rafters an owl squatted, its wings tight to its body and looking back at the men with its own wide eyes. The owl slowly opened its beaked mouth and released no noise, no screech, no warning.

Salvador climbed down quickly, and Place followed.

* * *

The early morning offered a teasing promise of a summerlike day. The clear sky blazed a clean, brilliant blue as the sun began its slow scaling of the eastern horizon. The usually cooling ocean breeze remained out to sea, and Place thought about the beauty of time and location. As he stood on the deck rolling up his sleeves, Salvador walked up to him with his usual deliberate steps.

"Buenos días, americanito. ¿Qué tal?" Place said.

"Bien, gracias," Salvador responded hastily. "Se salió un caballo!" And he pointed to Mickey's horse feasting on forbidden hay at the entrance of the hay barn.

"Mitch!" Place yelled as he took a last gulp from his cup of coffee.

Mitch emerged from the house pulling tight on her ponytail. "What a beautiful day," she said and then greeted Salvador.

"Look," Place said, pointing to Mickey's horse as it stood leisurely chewing and occasionally looking around.

"How did he get out?" Mitch asked.

And Salvador explained that he didn't know. He had found the gate opened only enough for the horse to escape, while Jacqueline's horse remained in the pasture, hesitant to leave its new habitat.

"Did anybody else get loose?" Mitch asked.

"No. No más el caballo de Mi-ke," Salvador answered quickly.

"That's strange," Mitch said. The trio walked toward Mickey's horse as they discussed how to pry him from his buffet of hay. Mitch carefully slipped the halter around the horse's head as it fidgeted like a little boy whose face is being scrubbed while distracted from what he had been doing. She looked at the tightly packed hay, and then looked out at the pastures she could see from where she stood. "It's so warm already," she said to no one in particular as she buckled the halter securely and began leading the horse back to its pasture. "Let's make the rounds. I want to check the gates and fences."

The two donkeys, Gin and Tonic, grazed steadily, looking up only to see if Mitch or Place offered something more substantial. The ducks remained huddled in their safe, limited corner as they pecked the earth looking for nourishment. Mitch handed Place a bunch of carrots as she untied a plastic bag of carrot and cucumber peels, tomato cores, and limp lettuce.

"Keep those two brutes busy while I feed the ducks," she said. "And save at least two carrots for Joker."

Gin and Tonic pulled at the carrots stingily as they kept their greedy eyes on Place and wondered with them how many carrots they would get. They chewed hard and rapidly, and when they finished a carrot, they pushed against the wire fence and jerked their noses upward, demanding more.

As Mitch and Place walked to the end of the ranch, they checked the gates and inspected the fences for weak posts and loose wire. When they arrived at Joker's lonely corral, Mitch pointed out that he had not stretched his neck through the gate like a beseeching beggar as Gin and Tonic had. Joker was not grazing on the yellowing grass, either, and he had not greeted them with his usual, proud, long brays that he punctuated with a traditional "heeeee hawwwww." Mitch furrowed her brow and studied the surrounding bushes and trees. Joker stood facing south, toward Miwok Creek, and secretly snorted in low, private intervals.

Mitch swallowed slowly and, taking the carrots from Place, she entered the corral. "Here, Joker," she said as she seductively waved a fat carrot in front of his nose. She looked back at Place, who was scanning the trees along Miwok Creek.

"What's wrong?" Place asked. "Why doesn't he want the carrots?"

"I don't know," a concerned Mitch answered as she bent over to inspect the donkey's legs and hoofs. She ran a hand under Joker's belly, feeling for an injury, and grasping for a clue. "I don't know donkeys like I know horses. But listen."

In the shadowed banks of Miwok Creek, a toad croaked in long, mesmerizing messages that only those of his kind understood. "Is that frog bothering him?" Place asked.

Mitch did not answer, but shook her head to indicate that Joker's southern posture was not because of the announcing frog.

After dinner, Mitch decided to walk the ranch. She was not comfortable with Joker's odd behavior, and her discomfort made Place feel uneasy.

The shorter autumn days and the less intense and now shy sun bowed to darker fall nights and a more enduring, overbearing moon. The horses stood still in their pastures and only reached down nonchalantly to nibble on the carrots Mitch threw to them. Gin and Tonic paced nervously along the fence, poking at the wire and examining Mitch and Place for carrots. The ducks nestled in their safe scoops of dirt, murmuring cautiously as they faded into a crisp night of sleep. On the deck of the ranch house, Rosa and Coquette stood in guarding poses only watching Mitch and Place and not following.

When they reached Joker's pen, they stood at the gate and observed as the animal continued to face south. Mitch shook her head as she had earlier that day, and Place knew that her brain was processing sights, sounds, and smells along with other events and signs that life had taught her were meaningful. Nothing in her mind fit the way she wanted it to. The carrots she had offered to the donkey in the morning remained on the ground, and Joker looked back at Mitch and Place, snorting and pausing. With each pause, Place wondered about Joker's snorting offer—it was one of conjecture, concurrence, and deep-running communication that he could not comprehend as much as he tried. He listened harder, trying to draw meaning from a mute, punctuated language: snort and pause, snort and pause.

The full moon shone down like a nocturnal sun, and the shadows of trees, fence posts, and phantom life froze into the ground. Moonlight blanketed Joker's back and revealed his brown markings on a white hide.

"You see how the markings run?" Mitch asked Place in a whisper. Place looked at the length of brown that started up by the donkey's head and broadened to a distinctive post all the way down to the animal's tail where it tapered to a point. At the shoulders, a transverse marking draped the donkey. Place had recognized that Gin and Tonic were marked in the same way.

"It's like a cross," Mitch continued. "And Joker, like Gin and Tonic, is really a burro. They're called Jerusalem burros because they're like the one Christ rode into Jerusalem. Some people still believe that all Jerusalem burros are descendants of the one Christ rode."

Joker shifted slightly as he lowered his head. Mitch threw a carrot to one side in an attempt to gauge some type of reaction. The burro stood in a hypnotic pose. Swirls of dry dirt fluttered into the air as he snorted close to the ground. Mitch looked into the silvery water of the donkey's trough as innocent ripples radiated from the center and bashfully kissed the sides.

In the early morning air, after a confusing night of restlessness, Place knew as he shoveled manure into a wheelbarrow that the sun would offer all of its energy to the fleeting day. The warm rays massaged his back and shoulders, and he breathed in the stillness of the ranch. Salvador walked quickly from the hay barn holding Gatita, and Place called out to see what had happened.

"Nada," Salvador replied as he gently tossed the cat in his house and slammed the door to ensure it stayed tightly closed. "¿Otro día de calor?" he asked Place as he walked to a pasture.

"I think so," Place answered. "¿Cómo está la Gatita?"

"She is very fine, thank you," Salvador answered and laughed at his own language.

Place dumped a final load of manure into the compost pit as Mitch walked out to the deck. She could feel that the unusual warmth would invite itself for another summerlike day, resisting the cool advances of a maturing autumn. With a silent stare, she focused on the overpacked hay barn. Wavy rays of heat filtered upward as if summoned by their source.

Mitch surveyed the land around her, not just of StarRidge Ranch, but of all the land she could see beyond and the land she could imagine beyond that. The countryside was unique to her because in spite of peopled growth and other questionable progress, there was an innocence and simplicity that she felt brought humans back to their real selves. When she thought about her relationship with animals, she realized too how the relationship between humans and animals was always a selfish but necessary one that fed the sybaritic impulses of the well-groomed and fashionably discriminating.

"What's up?" Place asked as Mitch approached.

"I'm going out to check on Joker. Want to come with?"

"Sure," Place answered. "Where are our faithful mutts?"

Mitch pointed a thumb over her shoulder and said as if she was confused, "They don't want to come."

"They're spoiled and lazy," Place said as he looked back at the deck where the two dogs maintained a unified Cerberean pose.

The couple walked up the dirt road and talked about the ranch. With Salvador's help, it was developing into a solid earthly citizen. The whiteness of the fences declared its sheer boundaries, and the landscape blushed with childlike nurturance. The bloated hay barn and the reconstructed milk barn showed signs of juvenescent life. The little help house that Salvador and Gatita shared and the ranch house that Mitch, Place, and the dogs occupied seemed to take on a deeper color just by the living contact.

From the distance, Mitch and Place could see Joker waiting for them as he extended his neck and head through the gate. His long ears pointed to the azure heaven, and his eyes probed their minds.

"Hi, Joker!" Mitch said excitedly. "You feeling better, boy?"

She offered the burro a carrot, and he chewed it with emphasis. He devoured the next carrot, and Mitch entered the corral to scratch his neck and sides while she examined him.

Place scratched at the animal's forehead and said, "Back to your old self, hey, Joker?" And as Place spoke, he knew that what he said assured him in some odd way.

Mitch looked down at Miwok Creek and walked along the fence of Joker's corral. Place stood at the corral entrance, hanging onto the fence. "He must have been drinking his water," he said. "His trough has little waves in it."

The soft breeze spread the heat of the sun along the land. Rosa and Coquette stood to greet their owners as they walked back from the other side of the ranch. Place scratched Rosa vigorously while Coquette nudged closer for her measure of attention. Mitch looked at the hay barn for a moment and then leaned back as she grabbed the railing of the deck. "Place," she started as her eyes widened.

Place felt a rumbling in his stomach and dizziness in his head. For a fleeting moment he thought about sunstroke, but realized it was only unusually warm and not the intensity of valley heat as he had known it. Salvador came running from one of the pastures, and without acknowledging Mitch or Place, he ran into his little house.

The hay barn swayed in a sleepy, swerving motion; the waves of heat floating and fluttering from the roof draped it in a bizarre and strange way. The ground rolled with the slow movement of a dream and thrust its pelvic pastures in an aching arc. The barns and houses cracked with loud pops as nails divorced wood and fence posts separated from the embracing wire.

Place tried to straighten, and when he did, he vomited. Mitch crouched low, still holding the railing as the dogs barked at the moving earth and ran under the deck. In a pasture, a swollen erection of metal burst up from the ground as a ruptured pipe ejaculated water wildly. Bales of hay crunched to the ground with gravitational thuds.

In his house, Salvador looked frantically for Gatita, and when he didn't find her, he pulled his mattress over his body as the earth continued to push up at him. The railing to which Mitch clung gave way, and she tumbled into the bushes. Place crawled to where she lay, and they held onto each other as the quake slid and jerked and shook their senses.

Place looked up at the three pine trees. They wavered unnaturally, making extreme arcs from side to side. He closed his eyes tightly, opening them again and hoping his vision would be more true. He held Mitch even more tightly, increasing his hug as the movement of the earth's magnitude seemed to intensify. In the distance, Mitch and Place could hear sirens that screamed from all directions. In the propinquity of bushes and splintered railings, they could feel the deep rumblings of land that was alive. After heart-throbbing minutes, Mitch pushed at Place and squirmed to release his grip, and they rose cautiously, hesitating on all fours as if feeling for the earth to move some more.

"Are you okay, honey?" Place asked, his voice parched with fear.

"Yeah. I'm fine," Mitch answered slowly and barely loud enough for Place to hear. "We better check on the animals and see if Salvador is all right."

Salvador emerged from his house almost crouching and stepping sensitively. He looked around suspiciously, and for a reason he did not understand, whispered forcefully in an attempt to call out to Mitch and Place. The couple approached from around the deck, and motioned to Salvador to follow them.

With a reciprocal whisper, Place said, "Come here. Ven pa'cá." Salvador stood low and frozen as he waited for the earth to shift and shake some more. "¡Ven pa'cá, hombre!" Place ordered, this time his voice more demanding although cracking in its disguised fear.

The three of them stood out in the middle of the lawn, away from structures and overhead wires. Salvador looked back at his little help house, and Place pointed out to him that a house, a home, a shelter, was the most dangerous place to be right now. Salvador responded that that was where his Gatita was. As he held back tears, he convinced himself that it was good that she should die where he spent many days bringing her to life.

They stared at each other like strangers as sirens wailed in the distance with intensity and desperation. Horizons became funneled with light and dark shades of smoke. Place looked at Mitch deeply, and his eyes asked confused questions. Mitch's attention was on the land. She methodically scanned the ranch as if her surveying was measured in quadrants. With each mental picture, her brain prioritized tasks, triaged sections of the ranch and situations of animals. Before fully acknowledging Place or Salvador, she prayed an apology to the earth of StarRidge Ranch.

Place looked at Mitch closely and wondered if she knew he was there. As he studied her he came to feel the calm strength she possessed, a strength that strangely made him jealous. There was a sense of respect she had for the land and what it could do, but there was also a piercing look that spoke of regeneration, of regrouping, of realizing they could do what they needed to do to help StarRidge Ranch.

Mitch finally broke the sweaty silence as she instructed Salvador and Place to turn off the water and gas while she checked on the animals. She rubbed her hands over her face as if to clean the fatigue and fear from it. "That long-eared prognosticator knew," she said, "and he tried to tell us."

Salvador and Place hurried to the water pump and propane tanks, turning spigots off as they took in the real damage to the ranch. The hay barn leaned drunkenly to the west; rafters and bales of hay were tangled in sprawled splashes. The once-proud fence lay flat in some areas, while other parts of it were bent upward and off the ground, forming an accordion of wooden posts and wire. From the middle of a pasture, the rigid pipe pointed accusingly at the sky. The two men walked to various pastures and corrals to check for gates that still worked and fences that still kept livestock in or predators out. Salvador swung a gate aggressively to show Place that some things still worked as they should. And as he swung the gate closed, it screeched with a plaintive meow. Salvador stared at the seemingly animate gate and then at the post that supported it. Crouched and cautious, Gatita meowed to him again.

"¡Mira, Plácido!" Salvador shouted, "¡Es mi Gatita!" And he reached down, picking his resurrected cat up by the nape of the neck just as her mother would have done had she known one. But like a proud father, he cradled her protectively and thanked God for saving her. The sunlight of a smile lit up the dark shadow of his moon-shaped face.

The smoke of faraway misfortune darkened the once-blue sky as Mitch walked to the other side of the ranch. Each step solidly announced to the ground below it that she, Place, and Salvador would mend the ranch, and they would only leave if human nature asked them to. Heading up the dirt road toward Joker's corral, she could see his antennalike ears and his wizardly expression.

He brayed hard and long with his nose pointed skyward, finishing with a humming, chanting trumpet of a blast for a god that only he knew. Then he looked at Mitch with sincere, wise eyes. She offered a carrot, and he continued to look at her as he crunched on the sweetness of the treat.

Over the phone, Mitch tried to convince, cajole, and persuade Jacqueline that everything at the ranch was fine. Of course they had felt a few tremors from the quake that had spasmodically sent the Richter scale into frightening motion, but really there was only a mild wave of movement felt in the neighborhood of StarRidge Ranch, and any damage could easily be fixed by Salvador and Place.

"Then why was your phone out for a few days?" Jacqueline asked, not feeling convinced, as she had witnessed the damage in her own home a hundred miles away.

Mitch ducked and darted into easy avenues of lies as she told Jacqueline that the county had been hit hard. The main highway into the county was passable in only one lane. Many other roads were closed and buildings declared off-limits because of their new instability. All of what happened in the urban areas, Mitch prevaricated, had a residual effect on the outlying areas and one of those products was phone lines that were temporarily down. "I don't think you can make it into the county, anyway," Mitch concluded. "The roads are locked up with rescue and repair vehicles and equipment, and the highway patrol is caravaning all vehicles because the Redwood Highway has only one lane open. It's been severed and sheared!" Mitch offered to keep Jacqueline apprised of new developments as they occurred, and for rhetorical effect added, "If any substantial aftershocks hit us, I'll call you the minute I can."

Salvador and Place had worked like Noah in their attempt at righting the listing hay barn. With the truck and rope, they pulled on leaning beams, and once straightened, they buttressed and reinforced precarious fractures and shored up debilitated rafters. Where the damage and remedial repairs looked too obvious, they stacked bricks, lumber, and other excess building material that Mickey had left. They hammered in the corrugated metal sheets of the roof using extra long nails. And when they had completed their task, they restacked the hay in a less ambitious configuration, keeping it closer to the ground.

Salvador and Place stood back from the hay barn and critiqued their efforts. Place tilted his head one way and then another as he tried to look to see how much the barn was slanting.

"Está parejo, hombre" Salvador assured him. "No te preocupes, mexicanito."

Mitch, Place, and Salvador worked steadily and patiently throughout the short days as they repaired fences, pasture sheds, deck railings, and wrenched gates. Salvador replaced the sprung pipe with material Mitch received from Sweet Wine Dairy in exchange for a day's labor. As soon as all immediate repairs had been tended to, coats of paint were applied to cover up any telling clues.

They welcomed evenings. They appreciated being able to rest and get ready for the following day. Each evening they sat outside and anxiously waited for the land to slide, collide, pinch, and punch. Under the desperation of their persistent labor, and concerned that Jacqueline and Mickey could show up at any moment, the trio sat in spent silence as they sipped on beers and gazed out at the sleeping ranch.

Place looked up into the viscera of the night sky. Cells of glinting stars hung in a noiseless broadcast of sempiternity. "A miner once told me that you can see the stars during the daytime," Place said as he continued with his face pointing skyward. "She said when you go down in a vertical mine shaft and you look up, the stars are there. They're always there. Stars always shine. And you can see them behind the blue sky." Salvador and Mitch did not respond, as he had expected, and he wondered about the name given to the ranch. The name didn't fit the property. The ranch was not situated on a ridge, or even a hill. It was a supine square of land that received more than it returned. Place followed a line of bright stars as they crested directly overhead. Along each side of the glistening line, dots of less luminous stars were scattered and Place could see invertible slopes of deep black marked by the less distinct dots of light. He focused more clearly on the ridge of stars as it pointed back at him.

In the following days, Place checked and rechecked the repairs they had made following the earthquake. He felt that he and Salvador had made the fences, barns, sheds, and gates as fit for ranch life as they had ever been. But he was not confident about the work they had done, and only time and nature would tell.

"It'll start raining soon," Mitch said, looking at Place's nervous face. "The rains will be a good test of the work we've done. I think everything will hold up nicely."

Mitch did not wait until the first of December to start providing feed for the animals, and she did not feed only the insufficient flake of hay that Jacqueline had measured with close hands. Coastal fog sauntered inland each night and remained for most of the morning, and now the animals needed fuel for those long, cold stands.

A drippy, dewy dampness chilled the air, and the striving sun beamed down with futility. Place's hands ached even more as he worked in the draft of the stall barn, carefully cleaning and painting individual walls and preparing each stall for its own tenant. The list of meticulous projects that Jacqueline had left kept Salvador and Place busy as the year gave up its final days.

Mitch looked out the kitchen window as the rain continued a dreary pace that had started in the dark hours of the night. The two horses hovered at the gate as they waited anxiously for their morning feed. Gin and Tonic butted the fence and gave short runs at the ducks in their anticipated nervousness for their first portion of the day. Mitch checked the clock, and with the strained waiting of the animals, confirmed that it was well past their feeding time. In a corner of the hay barn, Place methodically painted old shutters that Jacqueline had recovered from a yard sale and wanted attached to her new milk barn apartment.

"Has Salvador fed yet?" Mitch asked, interrupting the quiet daydreaming that Place was immersed in.

"Huh?" he answered as if someone woke him from a deep sleep. "What? I'm sorry. I was in the high Sierras, at my mountain ranch where the snow falls quietly and the steam from your breath tells you you're alive."

"Where's Salvador?" Mitch asked and added, "Has he fed yet?"

"I guess so," Place answered. "I mean, I assumed he had. Come to think of it, I haven't seen him this morning."

"Well, you better go check on him," Mitch said. "He might be sick or something."

Place knocked on the door of the little help house and waited. He knocked again, and then tapped at the front window calling out to Salvador, "¡Hey, americanito! ¿Qué pasa, hombre?"

"Estoy enfermo," Salvador replied through the door, his voice harsh and his tone abrupt.

"¿Necesitas algo?" Place offered as he moved closer to the door and put his ear up to it.

"¡No!"

"Okay, amigo. Pero llámame si necesitas algo. Voy a dar alimento a los animales," Place said and waited for a response.

"¡Ándale pues, guay!" Salvador lashed back, exuding obvious anger.

Place stood silent for a moment, shocked by the electricity of Salvador's words. He tried to make sense of them. He remembered that Salvador had once told him that in the winter he got sick and that there were days at a time when he couldn't work. Place had suggested that it was fatigue from the long summer days, and Salvador had assuredly but nebulously told him it wasn't. "¿Pues,

RICK RIVERA

cómo sabes?" Place had asked and offered that people could get the flu or a cold from working too hard. Salvador could only tell him he knew it wasn't from the usual winter ailments. As he walked to the hay barn to feed the animals, Place thought about his angry father. His father often abused the family with the same derisive tone that Place now felt from Salvador, and he felt those words down to the marrow of his sensibilities. They were words that hurt, and the users knew that words could do that. That words and language could sting, cut, and burn the spirit as much as a physical and frenzied beating could.

As Place slowly fed the anxious animals, he thought about Salvador and wondered how much he really knew about him. It had been so simple to assume that once a person helped somebody, he would in turn be grateful, thankful, filled with friendship. But Place knew enough from Mitch's litigious anecdotes that people were complex animals, and that part of that complexity was due to language, expression, and feeling. "The fact that we speak makes it hard for us to really know each other—and even harder to communicate," Mitch often warned Place as they lay in bed thinking about how they had only each other, never sure of even that. Place wondered if Salvador was happy, and then laughed inwardly as he tried to define for himself what happiness is or would be. He realized that with Salvador in his life, he felt more secure. It was a comforting network with Mitch on one side and Salvador on the other. Both accepted Place with his weaknesses and insecurities and both made him feel as if he were with his own people. But Place never considered that Salvador might aspire to more than being his coworker, or even his worker should Mitch and Place purchase their own small ranch. Place didn't consider that Salvador's goals might reach beyond being a ranch hand or migrant farm worker. In a way, Place's view of Salvador was very American, very Jacqueline.

"What did he say?" Mitch asked Place as he resumed his indoor chores.

Place thought for a quick moment. He wanted to lie, feeling both confused by the behavior of his companion and ethnically embarrassed. With each introduction to new ways of living, new ways of thinking, and new ways of doing things, Place became slowly resigned to the idea that all of his people were eventually what he was suspecting Salvador was and what he knew his own father had been. But Mitch had also taught Place that people couldn't be looked at like set items from a racial catalogue that has a description of characteristics and tendencies, batteries not included. She brought to Place's attention, on those few occasions when he slipped, that for him to think of his own father as being typical of a certain people was to do just what many people did when they thought about Mexicans, Blacks, Jews, Asians, doctors, ranchers, lawyers, farmers. "People aren't like that, Place, you know that," she would remind him.

"He's sick, like you said," Place answered as he carefully positioned a newly painted shutter off to one side to dry.

"What's wrong with him?" Mitch demanded, her training now talking as she sought out facts and taxied another question down the runway that launched answers toward the truth.

"I don't know," Place said and looked at Mitch with eyes that discouraged further questions.

Mitch knew because she knew people, that Place did not wish to talk to her about Salvador. She knew too what Place's volcano—sleeping but volatile—look could mean. It was a disturbing and detached gaze that did not frighten her for her own protection, but concerned her more for Place's well-being. It was that same eye-filled expression on a blank face that Place had once described to Mitch when he recalled the last day he saw his father. When she had seen that look for the first time and firsthand, she wondered desperately if Place knew he had inherited it. Out of patient respect, she never asked.

"Well, if he needs something, we can help him. Tell him that," she said as she walked away.

Place looked over at the ducks as he flung extra flakes of hay into Gin and Tonic's corral. It was important to feed the burros enough so that by the time he reached the other side of their piped-fenced yard, he could spread out the table-scrapped vegetables to the ducks and they could eat peacefully, if only momentarily. The ducks were smart. They knew to peck and pick at their meal while maintaining a careful watch on the rude roommates that were the two burros. They knew to waddle-run behind the safety of the surplus piping any time the burros felt the urge to charge at them, which was often. In their bowls of dug-out dirt, they roosted low and watched between the rails of pipe panels that leaned toward the more solid fence as they kept wary eyes on the two larger animals.

Place watched with rocks in his hands as the ducks came out shyly and cautiously like weary men shuffling to a soup kitchen line. He hurled rocks at the burros the moment they even looked toward the ducks, hoping that if he did that consistently, the long-eared pests would associate getting hit by a rock with looking at a duck. Place was mildly proud of the associative training he felt he had invented, although he never expressed this to

Mitch, and he was pleased that as soon as their extra work was caught up, he and Salvador would build a special little pen adjacent to the corral so that the ducks could have their own safe space. Place and Salvador had talked about it one day when they decided that the ducks seemed nervous and anxious like inner-city children who wonder when they will get caught in the crossfire of bigger kids, knowing it's only inevitable. The two men laughed suspiciously as they devised a way to make the new duck pen portable, so should Mickey and Jacqueline pull up unexpectedly, they could disassemble the pen quickly and inconspicuously and shove the ducks back in with Gin and Tonic where Jacqueline had mandated they should be. In their conspiratorial planning they joked and called Mickey and Jacqueline vulgar names—in English and Spanish, as if to deliver double-tongued curses.

The ducks ate quickly and Place urged them to slow down. They looked up at him as the scraps filled their throats and they honked half-quacks of satisfaction as they cleaned the ground of their afternoon meal.

"You're welcome," Place said as he doled out more peelings, cores, and crumbs.

He walked back to the deck and sat and watched as the hazy sun gradually turned into a semicircle and then went to another part of the world. The deck had become Place's mental observatory, the place where he could philosophically stargaze and wonder about the things that were important to him, the things that confused him, the things that hurt him. This evening's musing would focus on Salvador. He wasn't sure how to approach him, and the growing darkness with the slowly burning stars dotting its canopy seemed to calm him.

Place leaned back against the picnic table after drawing long and deliberately from a can of beer and looked for the star ridge he had identified weeks earlier. Lethargic clouds moved slowly toward the Sierras, and when Place thought about the mountains he remembered a recent day when Salvador and he had repaired a quake-damaged structure.

"¿Dónde está la sierra?" Salvador had asked as he scanned the ground scattered with assorted tools and looked for the saw.

Place, intrigued more by the language than by the question, asked "What's that? ¿Qué es un, uh, una sierra?"

Salvador explained to Place that "una sierra es a saw."

"¿Como las montañas?" Place had asked, uniquely interested.

"Sí, mexicanito," Salvador answered, "like las montañas."

This conversation led to geological speculation as Salvador and Place discussed the intricacies involved in naming the cragged peaks. Place suggested that the mountains couldn't be properly named the "saw mountains," and Salvador agreed. With meticulous analysis they studied the saw, turning it upside down so that its teeth pointed upward like a neat row of tiny mountains. Place continued, "In English, they would have to be the 'saw-tooth mountains.' That sounds better." Salvador, not really understanding the words and responding more to the tone, replied with his usual accommodating "Yes, mexicanito, es better." But their linguistic observations didn't end with that compromise as Salvador asked what "teeth" were. Place jokingly replied, "What you don't have too many of," and then immediately retracted the joke as possibly a hurtful one and one better left unexplained. Again they studied the saw as Place showed Salvador that the word "teeth" was used to describe a saw and also teeth in one's mouth. Together they marveled at the strangeness of words. Salvador added a footnote that in Spanish, only animals and people had teeth—not saws.

Place stared deep into the patches of silvery-dotted black as clouds continued to open and close the night sky like horizontal curtains. The hypnotic stillness of his nocturnal gazing lulled him into a peaceful rest as he slowly started to fall asleep.

Place wasn't sure if the dull thud he heard was from a dream. He opened his eyes slowly but wide in an attempt to sharpen his senses. The thud thumped once more and in a cymbalic crash the piping from Gin and Tonic's corral came smashing down. Place was slow to react as he stood at the railing of the deck and looked out toward the corral. The nighttime shadows revealed to him the two burros darting and skidding, raising their front legs high and coming down hard on round bodies of feathers. A muffled quack, one stomped and cut short through death, burped out and evaporated as it reached Place's ears. He ran toward the corral and behind him he could hear Mitch running along the deck. As he reached the corral gate, one of the burros chased the sole-surviving duck. As it smashed headlong into the wire and bounced back, the burro stomped it and its mate came to join in on the stomping like Nazi youth beating a solitary figure solely for being different. The duck rose once and with a deformed waddle scooted forward and sideways closer to the fence. A webbed foot jutted out at a perpendicular angle as the struggling duck fell forward with each inching movement. Its neck lunged ahead of it as if to take desperate steps or futile grasps as it propelled itself along the fence, receiving random stomps and obnoxious nudges from the fascist burros. As Place spanked the wire mesh fence with his open hands, he yelled a harsh "Yaa! Yaa!" and cursed words to beings that did not hear him and did not care.

Place and Mitch stood dumbly as they looked at the dead ducks, their bodies flat in the places where hoofs had stamped into them. Slowly moving blood crept in multidirectional spokes from the hubs of their bodies, and in an odd way showed that in death there are signs of life. Quietly, Place walked to the barn to retrieve a wheelbarrow as Mitch entered the corral and scooped up the birds with a shavings rake. Gin and Tonic paced nervously as they walked the trail of blood along the fence left by the last struggling duck. They reared their heads back snorting occasionally and jutted their necks forward and upward as if to salute an invisible power. They kicked out behind themselves in a daring gesture announcing personal space and took high, exaggerated steps to declare victory and ownership of a small country of land that was now *their* corral.

Place walked like a zombie as he pushed the wheelbarrow to a potential gravesite. His tears were angry ones, and he gulped damp, foggy air as his breathing grew jagged. Rosa and Coquette eagerly pranced alongside the wheelbarrow, smelling fresh blood and anticipating a vulturous meal.

Mitch followed closely, and quietly she asked, "Place, where are you going?"

"I'm going to bury these poor losers, if that's okay with you, Michelle."

"Place, let's not bury them," Mitch started. "Let's take them down to Miwok Creek. We'll just throw them along the creek. They died in a bad way and it's better if we let something else at least have their flesh. You don't want to bury contaminated souls."

In the quiet darkness of Miwok Creek, Place and Mitch stood and stared into the coagulated vein of semi-still water and thick earthly flesh. Slow steam rose from the heaped and still warm bodies of the destroyed ducks and behind the fences of StarRidge Ranch, Rosa and Coquette whined for their blood. Place reached into the wheelbarrow carefully for each body and respectfully laid them along the bank of the creek. Silently, Mitch prayed for the ducks—and for Place too. Quietly and quickly they climbed back over the fence and into Joker's corral. They stood at the fence as they stared down toward the creek just as Joker had done when he had anticipated the earthquake. In the thick night, Place and Mitch could hear cautious quadrupedal steps and the ripping of flesh as others benefited in a much more natural way from the deaths of the ducks.

Mitch stroked Joker's neck gently and turned to head back toward the house. "He's a gentle one, a less anxious one because he doesn't live with others," Mitch said as she and Place walked down the dirt road with the two dogs tentatively behind them. "It's good to live alone with just those who know you or at least try to know you."

"We gotta do that, Mitch," Place said sadly as he wiped his nose with a sleeve. "We gotta live alone, honey."

I n the chilled early morning, Place sat frozen like a barn cat waiting for a gopher to blindly poke its head through the freshly dug earth and into the unsuspecting air. He watched intently, waiting on the deck for Salvador to emerge, and started toward Salvador's home when the front door wavered and Gatita slithered through to take care of her morning business. As he approached Salvador's house, he could smell the stale drunkenness that reminded him of his father's lonely room, a room off limits to the family when their father was muy enfermo.

"¿Pues qué te pasa, hombre?" Place yelled after knocking on the fluttering door. And not waiting for a response, he shoved the door open like a cop without a search warrant. "Salvador!" he shouted as he stood with fists clenched, but not sure why.

From the bedroom, he could hear Salvador slowly rustling about, seemingly struggling to make his way to the living room. He could hear a bottle plop to one side and slide across the floor from an inadvertent kick, and Salvador emerged to face Place evenly.

Place knew, and at the same time he had hoped that what he suspected wasn't true. "Too drunk to work, Mexican?" he said in his finest commanding English.

Sheepishly, Salvador looked back at Place and uttered a piti-ful, "Yesss. Sí, hermanito. Too borracho para trabajar."

"Stupid Mexican!" Place shouted as he lunged toward Salvador, grabbing him by the front of his already torn shirt. "You have no right! ¡No tienes derecho, cabrón!" he continued. "Now that you have your green card, you think you can be like us, like any other wasteful American or mournful Mexican?" And not waiting or allowing for Salvador to understand or even answer, Place stepped closer to his bleary-eyed foe. "Get your things and get off this ranch! We tried to help you, you dumb-ass mule, and this is what you want to do with your life? Well, you'll do it somewhere else!"

Place turned quickly, and with the movement of a martial artist, he kicked the dangling door from its only hinge of support and walked toward the hay barn to feed the animals.

Salvador followed Place and attempting to offer a plea, began, "Por favor, Plácido—"

Place turned on him with tight fists and snarled, "Come on, Mexican! You want chingazos, that's the only other thing I can give you, and the only thing you people seem to understand."

Salvador stood straight, not flinching, not defending, but ready to take his punishment, and he dolefully explained to Place that he was an alcoholic. Dreary days made him feel desperate. He missed his family. He missed his country. And his music lured him to drink. To feel the sadness of his situation, who he was, who he might be, and where he might be going was something he knew Place couldn't completely know. How could Place know? he asked. Place was a lucky one. He had the suerte to be born in this coun-try. He could move between cultures but have the benefit and the citizenship of the one that mattered more. The one that was more valuable. Salvador could only have that with an envy-colored card that always reminded him he was only a corralled member of this society. Stamped for approval, if only on a limited basis.

"Lo siento. I sorry, Plácido, y me voy prontito."

Place threw the flakes of hay at the animals, hating them for reasons he could not explain to himself. "Eat shit!" he yelled at them as they ducked and dodged and cowered in confusion, poking at the feed as if under fire. He wanted to blame somebody for the futility that he and those like Salvador felt and lived. He was embarrassed for dreaming what he now saw as stupid little dreams, realizing too that that was the only place his voice was really heard—in those stupid, little, drunken dreams. He heaved an overabundance of feed at animals that were both hungry and cautious.

"What's your problem, Place?" Mitch asked as she stood a safe distance and calmly drew him around with the patient voice of a negotiator. "You don't have to treat these dumb beasts like that. If you have a problem, I'll feed them."

Place faced Mitch with the same anger he had faced those whom he thought had wronged him in a world he felt was naturally unfair. He knew why he was angry with Salvador and he felt that Salvador now contributed to his mounting frustration and that StarRidge Ranch itself had an agenda aimed at defeating him. His anger at Mitch was based on jealousy, a jealousy that envied Mitch's composure, her ability to handle situations that made his stomach churn and his knees quiver nervously. And at times he felt that he was a parasite, clinging to Mitch because she was capable of doing the things for which he lacked the fortitude.

"I'm leaving, Mitch. I've got to leave this ranch for a while. And if I don't come back, there's always another Mexican who can step in and do the work. We're everywhere, like cockroaches," he said and dropped a flake of hay as he headed for the ranch house.

"Are you leaving to do the same thing your father did to himself?" she asked, her tone detached, but knowing that the question would pierce Place's anger and make him think about what he always claimed he wouldn't be or do.

"Don't worry about it, Michelle!" Place sneered as he walked past her.

"Place, I'm not doing anything to hurt you and you know it!" she said. "I understand a lot more than you think I do. I'm not culturally ignorant, and I'm not against you."

"I don't care!" he shouted back as his stride grew more deliberate. "I'm tired of this ranch, and I'm tired of people like you.
You know, you're confident because people look at you expecting
you to be confident. Those same people look at guys like
Salvador and me and they expect us to be subservient and desperate. They see our ridged noses and round faces with big,
scared eyes, and we just look like hired help." Place felt good that
he had said that. He justified his thinking and his anger by recall-
ing what people had told him, never realizing what their
messages said, or never wanting to realize. He remembered the
professor in college who told him not to worry about finding
work because "if anything, you're the right complexion." But in
the end, it wasn't true. Things didn't really happen the way many
angry Anglos said they were happening. Jobs weren't really being
taken away from them to be given to swarthy people. It was a
world of connections, and to be connected professionally was
much better than being connected spiritually. Relying on your
own goodness and hard work, and hoping the universe would
reciprocate, Place had come to realize, wasn't a smart thing to do.
There is no law of reciprocity, as one minister had suggested to
him in a preemptive and encouraging moment during a time of
posthumous and paternal mourning.

As Place approached the deck to the ranch house, Rosa and
Coquette scurried from the anger they could sense. Peering from
a cautious distance, both dogs tilted their heads in confusion.

Place wept heavy tears of regret. Regret for who he was,
about which he was never really sure. He threw random clothes
and his father's gun into a box and strode from the ranch, heading north on Sweet Wine Road. His father had walked down a
country road on his last day. It now seemed easy to Place. Just
walk till you get there and wait for God or the devil to claim you.
They know how to sort things out.

Place walked the right angles of the road, feeling a sense of
relief and appreciating the free, unrestricted air. He considered
the box of clothes he had blindly gathered, and after a few more
moments of peripatetic thinking, he grabbed the gun and stuffed

it into his belt. He dropped the box of clothes, and continued to walk into a nebulous distance.

Place's itinerant migration led him down the reflective road. He shivered with guilt as he thought about Mitch and the ranch, and his fleeting thinking bucked him from extreme paths of indignation to empty arenas of remorse. He walked hard, each step a defiant kick at the earth that he now hated. As he turned another right angle of Sweet Wine Road, Place surveyed an old tree that had withstood the actions of men and Mother Nature, and shaded those who came to rest at its sloping, sheltering trunk. Salvador and Gatita sat at the bosom of the trunk and silently watched Place as he slowly discovered them.

Salvador stood respectfully, as if welcoming Place into his new home. He could see from the way Place walked as he approached the tree that Salvador and Gatita nested under that he was leaving StarRidge Ranch. Salvador could see too in Place's detached gaze, a gaze aimed at the road in front of him, that only Place knew of his destination. His eyes seemed to indicate that his mind had turned off, and with it so had his heart. Salvador stared at Place with clear and honest eyes. When he noticed the gun in Place's belt, he gulped slowly and nodded at it to wordlessly ask why Place would have such a thing with him.

Salvador apologized to Place again and explained that he was resting before moving on. He reached down to grab his own box of clothes and with Gatita faithfully following, they continued walking down Sweet Wine Road.

Place called out to Salvador, and when he turned around he asked him where he was going.

"Pues, no sé, Plácido," Salvador answered, and explained that he came to this country with no place to go, no place to belong. So things weren't much different from what he had experienced before. As he spoke, Salvador walked back slowly toward Place. He told Place that in spite of his ignorance, it seemed to him that one of the most regrettable things a person could do was walk out on his family. Salvador pointed to himself and explained to Place that yes, he was walking out on a lot of responsibility because he had made a mistake, but his family, his Gatita, was with him. It wasn't a good thing to be alone, Salvador offered.

Carefully he suggested to Place that he needed to go back to the ranch to help Mitch. He apologized again for his drinking and for any other trouble he might have caused and asked Place for one more chance. With a calming wisdom he explained to Place that they were all tired and frustrated. It was like the earthquake. The earthquake didn't happen to hurt people; there just happened to be people where the land shook, rolled, and waved. The earth is just tired, he explained, and so were Mitch, Place, and he. What made it more difficult, Salvador continued, was that they were working land that would never belong to them and it had always been that way. Place listened uneasily as Salvador spoke to him about the life of his people—their people. It was a futile existence; they both knew that. It didn't matter what side of the border you came from. For some reason, God didn't like them as much as he liked other people. But that didn't mean they simply quit living or trying. In fact, the more we try, Salvador suggested, the more we might win God's favor. But the worst thing they could do, he continued, was to just leave as both of them had now done.

Place breathed heavily as he stared at Salvador. Gatita now stood close to the tree, watching both men and waiting for them to move one way or the other. Softly, Place said, "Vámonos," and turned back toward StarRidge Ranch with Salvador and Gatita following silently.

Place slid into the ranch house quietly. He walked from room to room looking for Mitch, and when he didn't find her, he stepped out onto the deck.

Mitch sat at the picnic table with Rosa and Coquette positioned on either side of her. She looked over at Place casually and smiled slightly. Her expression exuded understanding and with it she seemed to allow for the frustration they were all feeling. Place stared for a few moments as if to study Mitch's profile. He wondered why they had ever met, and he concluded that it meant something more than just a relationship that eventually fizzles into the dull embers of familiarity and convenience.

"What are you doing?" Place asked politely yet curiously.

"I'm looking at the stars," Mitch answered as a lone tear streaked down her face. "Stars always shine, remember?"

Place sat beside her as Rosa and Coquette jockeyed for his new affection. Silently they stared out at the panoramic pastures of StarRidge Ranch. Mitch squeezed Place's hand tight and Place nuzzled his head on her shoulder. Quietly he offered, "But you can't see them from here, honey."

"I can imagine them from here," Mitch answered.

* * *

The winter rains continued to soak StarRidge Ranch as the new year broke quickly and the short days offered only brief intervals of opportunity to repair what the water had damaged. In the sloping pastures, rising waters flooded and receded, and when the sun broke through, Salvador, Mitch, and Place moved quickly to stabilize a fence post or move livestock to drier stalls and pens. Thick, impersonal fog moved in on some days and lounged like an annoying house guest, bringing with it its own dispiriting attitude.

After weeks of hard rains that rose to form impromptu ponds and flashing rivulets, a blanketing fog hid the land or smothered it like a firm hand over a muted mouth. Occasional appearances by the now stunted sun were ineffectual, and StarRidge Ranch sat like a tired mother.

Salvador puckered his lips as he studied the ranch. Looking closely at sleepy bushes, he pointed out to Place that some of the plants were starting to offer springtime buds. He sniffed the air the way Rosa and Coquette were used to doing and concluded that there would be an early and prolific spring.

"La primavera va a llegar con un gran besote," he said assuredly as he described how the change in climate would greet them and the ranch with a loving kiss. Flowers would bloom, babies would be born, and that was an indication and an invitation that the land would tolerate them for another cycle.

Place relayed Salvador's forecast to Mitch and she smiled cautiously as she watched horses react to the changing weather by dipping their heads playfully and kicking out at nothing in celebration of the coming season. Courting pairs teased one another with flirtatious, coy movements, the male of the pair offering a frolicsome love bite and then prancing away in a garish gavotte. He, his movements indicated, was a strutting and swaggering swain, a young man of a horse ready for a more mature man's world. Mitch smiled shyly as she studied the female of the couple responding with a marish squeal that indicated both pleasure and dispassion, a not-quite-ready yearning that warned her to be cautious of her would-be suitor. Mitch thought about the relationship between herself and Place. Place really was more like the mare, and she, Mitch, was more like the uncut yearling, or at least one that might be proud cut, who initiated the action, the motion, the sense and exuberance of living in a world that was always alive—and always dying.

"Jacqueline and Mickey will be arriving along with the spring," Mitch said, her tone affecting one of succulent gossip. "She just called, and they want to move in as soon as possible."

Place wasn't sure how to react. He looked at Salvador to see if he understood, perhaps better than Place himself now did. Asking as if he wasn't sure he wanted to know, he said "Well, how soon's as soon as possible?"

"As soon as things are dry and there's no mud and the grass is green and the smells die down, and angels hover overhead singing of a joyous day of salvation," Mitch answered with a scoffing tone aimed at a distant and dense Jacqueline and Mickey.

"So what are we going to do?" Place asked.

"What do you want to do?" Mitch asked back. "We can tough it out with them hanging around and see how much we can take. It's up to you, Place. We can leave when we want to. We can find us a place, and one for Salvador too. We're doing okay. We don't need this ranch with them on it if we don't want to do that. Although, you never know, they might have changed, and for the better."

"You mean kind of like two old and obnoxious dogs that might have learned new tricks?" Place asked, his voice definitely skeptical and sharp.

"Well, yeah," Mitch said and offered, "You know, you *can* teach an old dog new tricks. I've done it. I always wondered where that saying comes from. But I trained an old, scruffy, dumb dog I picked up on a lonely highway to be a good house companion, so now I don't believe in all those supposedly wise tales and bits of sage advice."

"Are you talking about me?" Place jokingly asked and then looked over at Salvador, who laughed along with the couple, not really knowing what he was laughing at. Place had asked Salvador about that—how he could laugh when others laughed but not understand fully what the joke was. Salvador explained to Place that laughing was the same for all people. "Somos diferentes perros de la misma raza," he explained. Place liked that, and felt good that Salvador included him as one of the different dogs of the same breed. So they could all laugh together even if only two of them fully understood the reason for laughing.

"So think about what you want to do, Place," Mitch advised. "Let's just make sure we have our ducks in a row and we'll be ready when those two come up."

"But what about Salvador?" Place asked as he pointed to his coworker.

"He'll be okay," Mitch assured. "I can find him a place where he'll be treated just fine. Remember, he has letters of recommendation. I'll make it so that his Gatita will be able to go with him. Tell him what's going on."

As Place and Salvador walked toward the hay barn to prepare the irrigation hoses for another season, Place explained the impending gloom of Jacqueline and Mickey's move to the ranch. They talked about Jacqueline and Mickey's ways. They tried to figure out the pair and they did this by attempting to assign to their personalities qualities and quirks that they had seen in some animals they knew. Salvador began the analogy with a simple suggestion that they were like chickens. They weren't very smart, he reasoned, and their ideas for running the ranch were limited, like a chicken's ability to fly. They weren't deep thinkers, just as a chicken isn't a high flyer.

Yes, but they were like unbroken colts, Place countered. They needed schooling and training, and a young horse doesn't just naturally ask for it. They're fine being horses that don't know any better. As long as they have food and water, they don't particularly care if they're ever shod or their teeth are floated. They don't want to be ridden, anyway. That's all stuff humans have a need or want to do. Salvador nodded his head in agreement, persuaded by Place's logic. He then amended his profile by claiming that they were really two different animals. Mickey was really kind of harmless, Salvador observed, and he knew a lot. That new milk barn apartment was evidence of that. But in front of other people, especially Jacqueline, something happened to him. To show what he meant, Salvador stopped from unraveling the hoses and motioned to Place with his right hand holding onto an imaginary handle and turning it toward and away from his body. "Yes, you're right!" Place exclaimed. Mickey was the monkey and Jacqueline was the organ grinder. They laughed aloud as they inspected the hoses for needed patches, each thinking up more animal analogies for a conversation that had become a spirited sort of competition and a horse race of ideas.

That evening, as Place, Mitch, and Salvador sat on the deck sipping ginger ale, Place relayed to Mitch what he and Salvador had developed in their earlier conversation as a way of understanding Jacqueline and Mickey.

"But why would you try to compare them to animals?" Mitch asked with a puzzled sincerity. "It's funny how we try to characterize people with animal-like qualities. I think that's called anthropomorphizing. But it's really not fair to the animal. Animals aren't necessarily like what we think they are. That's just us giving them our labels because that's how we see things. And it's too bad we see things like that in animals. Although many times we're right to see those things in people."

Place was interested and wanted Mitch to continue. Salvador scanned the land as if in the reflective process of inventing more beastly analogies of Jacqueline and Mickey.

Mitch lectured while she stood leaning against the rail of the deck. She offered examples of the vulturous lawyers she had come across in her practice. Then she showed that even though she often referred to her colleagues in that manner, the comparison was a false one. "Real vultures," she explained, "feed on carrion. Things have to be dead, even decaying for them to want it. But litigious vultures don't wait for death; instead they initiate it in many forms. And then they still eat from it—dead and alive." Mitch offered more evidence and cited snakes in this example.

Mitch liked snakes. They were good and necessary creatures, and could be especially effective on a ranch. She explicated the flaws in calling someone a snake in the grass, and talked about how a snake has no choice but to be a snake in the grass or anywhere else on the ground. As she talked, she slithered an open hand through the cool night air. "So a snake in the grass isn't necessarily predatory without reason to be, you know. But people are, and many times, without reason to be. Just to be." She paused to let Place think about what she had said. She continued by asking, "I've told you about that gopher snake I've seen in the hay barn?"

"Yeah, I've heard about it," Place said, not really as interested in or enthused about snakes as Mitch was. "I haven't seen him yet, and I don't want to."

"Ah, but he's a good fellow," Mitch said. "He knows you don't want to see him. He's the one who gets all those mice and gophers you don't like. Which would you rather have?"

"Neither," Place answered quickly.

"Yeah, in a perfect world, huh?" Mitch responded, her voice indicating she was a reasonable person who understood the way things were. "Anyway, my point is that animals don't have the characteristics that humans do. Ma Nature is good and she knows what she's doing. Humans are so varied, so strange, so perverse, so disorderly in a world where we want order. It's not our eyes that play tricks on us, it's our brains. Animals don't do that. They don't abuse their young. They don't kill for trivial reasons. They aren't necessarily mean, unless we've had a hand in their development. Actually, we're a lot like them because we're just trying to survive, although I don't think we know how to do that as well as they do."

"Yes, ma'am," Place answered as he mocked Mitch's passion for the subject she had delivered in the tradition of great orators. He instructed the ruminating Salvador to say the same but only in his language, and Salvador respectfully responded with "Sí, señora." The two men laughed a brotherly laugh like boys who sit at the back of a classroom and make fun of the teacher.

"Well, you two jokers can think about what you want to do," Mitch said, smiling slightly at their little teasing game. "We have some time to think about Miss Jacqueline and Monsieur Mickey. Her call was like a falcon, towering in her pride of place. And I'll let you guess whose line that is," Mitch concluded as she teased Place with his own passion for Shakespeare and the strangeness of human nature. Then, talking rapidly so Salvador would not catch her words or her meaning, she said to Place, "There are a couple of other things I want to talk to you about that relate to him. And don't give away anything by looking over at him. Just wait."

They retired for the night, weary from the day, each anxious to enjoy a deep sleep like hibernating bears.

lace's abrupt manner confused Salvador, and at Place's urging, the two men worked fast at measuring out lengths of hoses and deciding which pastures they belonged in. Occasionally Place flashed mysterious, sneaky, even seductive glances at Salvador, glances made more enigmatic by the surreptitious smile that accompanied and adorned the forecasting yet foggy face. Salvador worked quickly and quietly as he wondered what Place was up to.

Finally, when Salvador could wonder no more, he asked Place if everything was all right.

"Todo está bien, americanito," Place assured him and then added in mocking English, "To-morr-ow, we no worky. You comprende?"

Salvador considered Place's message and question carefully. Something about the tone seemed mean-spirited, taunting, and not fully clear. Why Place was acting strangely was a question that wound its way through the undulating canyons of Salvador's brain. Each time, the question backed out of one gray crevice and tried another, only to yield to dead ends that revealed nothing significant, the answer securely garaged in Place's occult thoughts and behavior. The effect caused Salvador to take his cap off and scratch his head, digging into his skull to dredge up a clue.

"¿Pues qué te pasa contigo, Plácido?" Salvador finally asked, feeling left out of a private joke that Place shared with only himself.

"I'm happy. Estoy contento," Place answered as he raised a flirtatious eyebrow and teasingly blew a kiss toward his friend.

Salvador ducked as if to avoid a boxer's jab and shied away from his suddenly peculiar partner. He thought about the changing weather and how the springtime caused people and animals to behave in different ways from what their natures usually dictated. As Salvador searched for a meaningful explanation, he realized how little he knew about Place. He knew factual things like where Place was from, what he had done, and where he had been, but these things revealed nothing more than strangers do when conversing at a bar or a bus depot. Salvador had only a superficial knowledge of his friend and he compared it to the basic things a young wife might know about her new husband.

What further confused Salvador about Place and what he might be was the ineffective discussion they had one evening when Salvador had asked Place what a Chicano was.

"A Chicano?" Place asked, answering Salvador's question with his own question, surprised that Salvador did not know what a Chicano was. He started cautiously, making up a definition as he went along. "A Chicano es como un mexicano americano."

"¿Y cómo son diferentes?" Salvador asked.

Place, stumbling on his own ideas as he tried to recall what he had once read years earlier, asked, "¿No sabes qué es un chicano?"

"¿Pues cómo voy a saber?" Salvador asked and then added, "En México no tenemos chicanos."

"What?" Place asked, surprised at the news. "What do you mean you don't have Chicanos in Mexico?"

"No, mexicanito. No tenemos chicanos en México," Salvador repeated. "No más mexicanos. Pero aquí tienen chicanos y también tienen mexicano americanos. Y creo que son diferentes. ¿Cómo lo ves?"

Place wasn't sure how he saw things now because he had never thought about Chicanos, Mexican Americans, and the differences that Salvador thought there must be in the two. "Well," Place started, distinctly confused by Salvador's inquiry, "Un chicano tiene una causa."

"¿Qué es la causa?

"Well," Place tried to continue, certain that what he was explaining made him uncertain. "La causa es que los chicanos quieren la tierra que era de ellos pero se la quitaron los americanos." Place nodded with some assurance, feeling good that he was able to offer a nebulous explanation and hoping that Salvador would now change the subject to irrigation or feeding the animals.

"¿Qué tierra?" Salvador asked, wanting to know more about usurped land.

"Aztlán," Place said, not offering further details because Salvador had now dragged him into unfamiliar territory. In a way this made Place feel guilty as well as uncomfortable.

"¿Dónde está Aztlán?" Salvador continued.

"Cerca de México," Place responded. "I think. Cerca de Tejas," he continued as he amended his answer.

"Pero Tejas y mucho de esa tierra era de nosotros," Salvador said and pointed a thumb to his chest, explaining that there must be some confusion regarding who owned what land and when. "Mucho de la tierra de los Estados Unidos era de México y de los mexicanos, no de los chicanos."

Place shook his head and relented that he really didn't know about Chicanos, Aztlán, or who had owned Texas or any other states. And he wondered why that was. He scratched lightly at the side of his face, feeling alienated from what he felt might be part of his own identity. "I don't know," he said. "No más sé que soy mexicano americano y no soy chicano."

Salvador, not really knowing any more about Place except that at that moment he was confused, suggested that one day they would find a Chicano and he could explain his own identity to them. He further suggested that one day perhaps he and Place could travel to Aztlán to see what it was like.

"Yes," Place answered, grateful that the discussion was ending as the night grew cooler, "one day we'll go to Aztlán. Good idea, americanito."

As Mitch served the two tired men their dinner, she spoke deliberately to Place, not directing him to explain anything to Salvador about the next day's events. Her words spilled out quickly in an effort to throw Salvador off from catching a clue to her plans.

"First, you'll take him to the feed store to buy him boots and jeans. And make sure you get him the good leather roper boots and the boot-cut jeans. Get him a long-sleeved, colorful cowboy dress shirt too, the kind with a yoke. I'll wrap his belt and we'll give it to him at lunch," Mitch instructed. "He's going to be sitting like a big dog when we go out tomorrow evening. Your clothes are hanging in the closet, and I want you to try them on tonight to make sure they fit nicely. I picked up your boots from the bootmaker this morning, so make sure you try them on too. They do look mighty fine," Mitch added with an impressed tone, as if reminiscing about a past lover. "When you get back from shopping," she continued, "we need to be ready to go to lunch. I have everything arranged at the restaurant. And then we have to be at the Boot Hill Bar by four o'clock."

Place nodded knowingly to signal to Mitch that he understood how the schedule was to proceed. In the early morning, they would wake up Salvador with "Las mañanitas" and an elegant, deeply dark chocolate cake with candles displayed in a question mark.

Upon reviewing Salvador's papers in preparation for a possibly impending move, the bogus documents and the real ones, Mitch had discovered that his birthday was nearing and it was only fitting that some celebration was in order. Of course, she realized that the date could be misleading, but it didn't matter because Salvador often indicated that he wasn't sure when his birthday really was. It was also better that way for Mitch and Place in terms of the element of surprise, as Salvador did not seem to acknowledge that his birthday was soon.

Place had continued to throw his friend off any suspicious trails by telling Salvador that they would need to spend the next day running errands around the county. Building material had to be picked up here and a dump run had to be made there. But it was easy work as Place explained it, so it was really like a day off.

In the cool spring morning air, Mitch walked carefully toward the help house with her question-marked cake. At the back distance of the ranch, in the corralled boundary nearest Miwok Creek, Joker wailed as his bray bugled reveille and his snout saluted the morning sun, announcing to tenants and neighbors of StarRidge Ranch that another day of active duty was beginning.

"That damn Joker is going to tip him off," Place jokingly whispered as he quickly positioned the tape player next to Salvador's front door.

Mitch instructed Place to knock on the door as she lit the candles while balancing the cake on the faded white fence that made up the borders of the help house.

Place knocked hard and fast and yelled menacingly into the door, "¡Abre la puerta; aquí viene la migra, americanito!" And Mitch raised questioning eyebrows at Place's teasing threat that the border patrol was on its way.

Inside, Salvador opened his eyes quickly and Gatita's eyes snapped wide to form big, round orbs, both of them now fully awake at the sudden pounding. Salvador jumped into his worn jeans like a fireman responding to a call and as he zipped them, his quick fingers were stopped by the melodic birthing of a familiar tune. Slowly, "Las mañanitas" pushed through the front door and seeped through the living room window and delivered itself to Salvador's ears. He walked toward the door as if in a trance, his legs heavy and moving forward in circumspect steps; they were exploratory probes. The tune picked up in tempo, emerging from the womb of the old recorder like a bloody newborn baby who cries for life when first exposed to the outer world of humans with expectations.

Salvador opened the door, and Place lunged at him with a hug that was long and lasting.

"¡Feliz cumpleaños, cuate!" Place yelled as he held tightly to his dear friend. "Tú siempre serás mi amigo," he continued, as he whispered to Salvador an oath of eternal friendship.

"Happy birthday, Sal!" Mitch cheered. And then in broken Spanish, as she held the cake in front of him to blow out the candles, "¡Fe-liz cum-ple-años!"

Salvador was stunned and remained silent, and as Place and Mitch urged him to make a wish and blow out the candles, he looked back at them and then behind them, still wondering if the border patrol was on its way.

On the deck, the trio ate cake and drank from mugs of steaming coffee, and Place rewound the cassette and played the Mexican birthday song over and over, occasionally asking Salvador what certain phrases meant. These early little mornings were young, innocent, and peaceful, and Place regretted that they often matured into days that required him to deal with their quirks, confusions, and confrontations.

Salvador sat respectfully and ate with caution as he stared at what was left of the cake. Without looking up he told Place he had never had a birthday cake. There was an apologetic sadness in his words, and they seemed to be burdened by a brooding sense of memory and loss. For Salvador, life was like a trinket, and he knew it should be worth more. But it was that trifling aspect of his own existence that had allowed him to take the chances he had, to meet people like Mitch and Place, and to believe that bigger and brighter trinkets could be his too. He sipped his coffee and wished he could disappear into its protective blackness.

Mitch, the one who paid more attention to the tradition of time on a watch or clock rather than what the sun declared, reminded Place that he and Salvador had some shopping to do.

"If you get confused, ask for Charlene," Mitch offered in the form of last minute instructions. "She'll know what you need."

At the feed store, Salvador emerged from the dressing room with stiffly creased blue jeans. His wrinkled work shirt hung loosely over his waist, and Place tucked his thumbs into the waistband of his own pants as a signal to Salvador to check the fit.

RICK RIVERA

"You need to put boots on," Charlene instructed as she watched with the discerning eye of a fashion critic. "That way you'll see if they hang the way they're supposed to. Never buy jeans without seeing how they fit with your boots."

Charlene walked quickly toward the boot section of the store with Place and Salvador following closely. After measuring Salvador's foot, she disappeared into a back room.

As they waited for Charlene to return, Salvador pointed out to Place that his jeans seemed too long. To prove his point, he stood up and showed him how the jeans dragged past his socked heel and covered most of his foot.

"Está bien así," Place assured him. "It's okay, you'll see."

Charlene's wiry body emerged from the back room, and in front of her she held a stack of boxed boots. She told Place how the boot should fit and he translated the instructions to Salvador.

Salvador stood straight and pulled up on his jeans. The boots lifted his pants off the floor, and even though they still looked long with only the toe of the boots bashfully peaking out from under them, they no longer dragged like a plow behind a tractor.

Charlene nodded her head in approval and motioned with her finger for Salvador to turn around. "That's sharp," she said with an analytical tone. "We get the right shirt on him and he's ready to go honky-tonkin'. Hell, I might want to go out with him," she joked as she winked at Place.

It was a shiny shirt with rays of colors that seemed to brighten Salvador's face. Red, blue, green, and yellow stripes picketed his torso and streamed down the long sleeves of his arms. Charlene tugged at his shoulders and pushed his arms up as if she were dressing a mannequin. She turned him as her keen eye studied his shirt, pants, and boots. Her smile showed satisfaction.

"He's ready," Charlene declared. "He only needs a belt and a hat and every cowgirl from Red Bluff to Bakersfield will turn her head to check this wrangler out."

Place told Charlene about the custom made buck-stitched belt Mitch had ordered with Salvador's name hand-tooled on it and a buckle which showed a ranch hand with his animals. He didn't bother to explain why they hadn't considered a hat and just mumbled to Charlene that the hats were on their way. But Mitch didn't like them, especially cowboy hats. As far as Mitch was concerned, hats were an expression of an overblown ego, and Place and Salvador didn't have that problem, nor did they need to assume it. Charlene expressed approval at the selection of the belt, and as she rang up the items she casually asked if they would need a bootjack.

"I hadn't thought about that," Place said, grateful for the reminder.

Charlene reached under the counter and produced a bootjack. As she continued ringing up the merchandise, Salvador picked up the bootjack and puzzled over it.

"¿Qué es esto?" He asked Place as he turned the item in his hands in an attempt to figure it out.

"It's for your boots, to take them off," Place answered as if Charlene had asked the question, and to make his explanation more clear he repeated himself in Spanish as he put the bootjack on the floor and guided the heel of Salvador's booted foot into it. He tapped at Salvador's other leg and told him to place his foot on the tail end of the bootjack. Helping him in a mechanical way, Place motioned for Salvador to pull up on the bootjacked heel. The new boot slid off smoothly, and Salvador looked at the simple contraption with awe. He placed his other booted heel in the device and pulled his leg upward. It was marvelous!

"¡Pinches americanos, tienen todo!" Salvador exclaimed as he stepped back into his new boots, impressed by American ingenuity. All the way home he examined the simplicity of the tool that helped a tired and solitary man take his boots off without sitting on the edge of the bed and yanking outwardly and awkwardly.

The food was colorful. Saucy reds and greens flowed into yellowy cheeses that melted over meats and beans. The orangeness of the rice added to the kaleidoscope of food. The blue-and-red corn tortilla chips mixed in with the traditional yellow chips indicated that indeed Mitch, Place, and Salvador were eating at an upscale restaurant. Carefully, Place and Salvador ate around the blue and red chips, together ignoring them for their odd color, but doing this only subconsciously. Mitch noticed this and thought to ask about it. But the more she ran the question through her head the more aware she became of what such a question would imply.

"How come both of you are ignoring the blue and red chips?" she thought to ask, and then decided against it, thinking the question too ethnocentric, too much like anthropology. That mental question collided with the other one she always wondered about: "How do you pick which language to use when you're speaking with other people who also speak both Spanish and English?" Mitch had asked Place about that linguistic switching, but he was vague in his answer, unsure himself. Mitch studied the two men as they ate and listened closely as they spoke, even though she understood very little of their casual conversation.

They ate like Romans. With few words spoken, they slowly consumed all of the food placed before them. They traded portions of the main course. A couple of spoonfuls of chile colorado for the same amount of chile verde. Mitch's plate of carnitas proved to be an effective trading commodity as she negotiated a deal for Place's cup of soupy beans, frijoles de olla. All parties involved in the trading ate with satisfaction, eating as if the food would provide needed energy for hard-worked bodies and tired minds.

Salvador took an indulgent drink of his ginger ale, sucking on the straw until the sounds of the empty glass gurgled and chuckled that the resource had been fully tapped. He sat straight and put a fist to his mouth to let a suppressed burp filter through. Place took a finishing swipe at his plate with a piece of flour tortilla, and Mitch continued to enjoy her meal, focusing on the bright mound of rice.

As the trio placed utensils and napkins on empty plates and pushed them away to indicate that they were finished eating, Mitch shot a warning glance to Place and he nodded with a pokerfaced knowledge that signaled that he was on cue. Place reached across the table to shake Salvador's hand and wish him happy birthday once more. With his other hand coming out from under the table, Place extended a small, brightly wrapped box toward him.

Salvador's eyes lit his face, and before opening the box, he thanked Mitch and Place for the thoughtful birthday they had arranged. He reminded the couple about how they helped him become a legal resident—of sorts—how well they worked as a crew, and how he had never had such caring friends. He redirected his encomium to specific examples and explained how each was effective in promoting friendship and a sense of belonging. "Somos parejos," he declared, but continued in this direction for only a short way. Place cut him off abruptly as he urged Salvador to open his gift.

Salvador apologized and unwrapped his gift. His rough, thick, dirt-dark fingers pulled at the blazing wrapping paper as if he were peeling a banana; he was delicate in his approach, and Place felt sorry for him, for his ignorance, for who he was.

The belt buckle gleamed against the darkness of Salvador's hands, and the hand-tooled leather belt uncoiled slowly as he examined the swirls and angled cuts of the oak leaf and acorn design with the buck stitching that ran from one end to the other, separated in the middle by his name in big block letters. The buckle shined like a silver platter, and Place joked to Salvador that he could always use the buckle as a dinner plato in case of emergency. But it was the scene on the buckle that captured Salvador's attention as he studied the etched lines. A lone figure leaned against a post-and-rail pasture fence, looking satisfied and secure with his arms folded. The long-eared head of a burro peered over his shoulder and a round cat sat at his feet.

Mitch invited Salvador to stand up and put on his new belt. His face grew warm as he moved shyly, threading the belt through the loops of his jeans with fumbling fingers. He glanced around the room to see if any of the other patrons was watching him, and he was amazed, almost disappointed, that nobody overtly observed him, but rather paid close attention to their own lives at that point in time. The belt buckle served as a glittering announcement that attracted the eye toward the blazing colors of the long-sleeved shirt, the distinct crease in traditional blue jeans with the rectangular leather tag sewn into a rear pocket that only those who had worked with livestock could proudly wear, and the low-heeled, round-toed boot canopied by the style and cut of the jeans.

The clothes offered a causal explanation of who the wearer was. They indicated a culture—a culture of work and of earning, and Salvador knew as he tugged at his pants and looked down at his new belt and then his boots, that he had entered into this other culture. He had earned membership, and in the swirls of smaller and varied groups that form a larger society, Salvador's new clothes gave him a sense of place. The clothes indicated that the wearer possessed a certain type of practical knowledge when working in fields and corrals, and that knowledge was acquired through doing, and from doing came learning. Production and self-worth followed, and a person could feel competent and complete.

Salvador did not show his surprise when he asked where they were headed as Mitch drove west on a country road and Place answered with, "Una cantina." He wanted to ask why, but decided to let patience eventually bring the answer to him. Salvador sat with his shoulders wedged between the door of the pickup and Place, who sat in the middle.

Mitch drove into the dusky parking lot of the Boot Hill Bar. The lot was full as tired workmen stopped off to unwind and talk and avoid other things before going home. Before they exited the truck, Mitch placed a hand on her husband's thigh and offered her unsolicited counsel. Place didn't like the idea of possibly having to ignore something somebody said, especially in a popular place like the Boot Hill Bar where fraternal men with hats that revealed more than they hid, swaggered, swore, and stroked women with silver-tongued words. Mitch further urged him to simply "study these types. You'll notice interesting things psychologically and culturally. Really, it'll be fun, Place."

As they walked toward the entrance of the bar, Place turned to tell Salvador, as if warning him, that the Boot Hill Bar was "una cantina de cowboys."

Salvador simply shrugged his shoulders, deciding once he discovered their destination that he would not mention to Mitch or Place that he knew all about the Boot Hill Bar and its friendly female patrons who skillfully knew how to separate working men from their money in exchange for the comfort of some company. He allowed destiny to guide his birthday celebration as it had guided the other events in his life.

Music galloped at them as they entered the bar. Loud talking competed with the volume of guitars, fiddles, steel guitars, and boxed voices that offered two songs for a quarter. Place and Salvador hesitated, stared at dust-worked cowboys as they stared back, and stood awkwardly for a few moments at the entrance of the bar as if waiting for a challenge of acceptance or exclusion.

When Place refocused his attention, he realized that Mitch was no longer standing next to him. In the farthest corner of the bar, across the shiny dance room floor, Mitch dipped her head as a shorter, stringier woman talked closely into her ear.

"Pleased to meet you, Miss Futtrell," Place said as Mitch completed the introduction between dance instructor and student.

"Mucho gusto," Salvador respectfully offered as he shook Rita Futtrell's soft, small hand and bowed his head slightly to offer a further hint of humbleness.

Mitch explained the plan to Place, who would then surprise Salvador with the news that they would learn the Texas two-step tonight.

"I'll have you cuttin' a rug before the evening is over," Rita Futtrell guaranteed. Then she yelled across the dance room floor to deliver a commanding order: "John, turn that jukebox off now, please."

Mitch smiled to herself as the bartender quickly pulled the plug on the jukebox, and a booming, boasting voice suddenly spiraled down from a high-pitched announcement to a lowly dying silence. Place was impressed, and he nodded his head in approval.

A lanky, coltish, young-faced cowboy with a wide-brimmed hat that made him look perpendicularly rail-like, smiled broadly as he approached Rita Futtrell with his petition.

"Now, Miss Futtrell, that don't seem too fair that I put two quarters in that box and I expect to hear some songs and enjoy a drink or two after a hard day and now you're turning it off."

"You'll have to listen to your songs later, Junior. I got paying customers who want to learn how to dance and I don't want that music interfering with mine," Rita explained with growing annoyance, her lips thin and tight revealing what Place considered as an okie-like overbite. "Now don't test me, boy. Tell John to give you a drink compliments of me and enjoy your buddies without the music."

Junior's face lit into an accepting and sincere smile as he slowly backed away from Rita Futtrell. "Can you at least put the pliers to your music, Miss Futtrell, so we can hear it over there?"

Rita said nothing as she turned and popped a cassette into her player and cranked the volume up enough for the music to escape the boundaries of the dance floor. Junior two-stepped across the floor without spilling a drop from his full glass of beer, which he held away from himself as if he danced with an imaginary partner.

"I *own* this place," Rita offered as Mitch, Place, and Salvador stood waiting and impressed. "When you're the owner you get to do things your way. Now, let's dance."

Rita Futtrell was more than just a dance teacher. She competed actively in dance contests and continued to be a student of movement and music and partners. She also read books and attended seminars and workshops. As a teacher, she enjoyed watching the growth and transition in those who came to her for instruction in moving with the music. Rita shifted from her introduction and began to talk about timing, knowing your partner, and feeling the tempo of the song to determine its "musicality and what you need to do to make sure you have a good sense of the rhythms of the songs."

"I'll start you off with a basic two-step," Rita said.

Place wasn't quite sure how to explain the more technical aspects of dancing to Salvador, so he told him in Spanish to simply do whatever he and Mitch were instructed to do.

Rita's fingers punched the recorder's buttons to advance the tape and then rewind as she searched for the right song. She instructed Place and Salvador to watch as she took the preliminary two-step steps. Taking long, sliding, slow steps, Rita Futtrell danced away from the corner of the unwinding music and started to follow the dance floor perimeter in a counterclockwise direction. "The rhythm is two-quarter time: step together, step together, step touch, step touch, step together, step together, step touch, step touch," Rita called rhythmically as she demonstrated with comments dispensed over her shoulder, increasing the distance between herself and her watching students. When she completed a circle and ended up back at the corner table where Mitch, Place, and Salvador were beginning to feel secure, she said, "Now the men will try it, but in a straight line. And by the way, when you do really dance and there are other people on the floor like there will be later tonight when the band starts up, you go in a counterclockwise direction."

Rita walked out to the dance floor and Place was momentarily mesmerized by her rapid short steps that caused her hips to switch rhythmically. "Just two-step out to me," She called to Place and Salvador. "But listen to the music to get your count. You need to know when to get on with your timing."

Place bobbed his head awkwardly and started hesitant lunges as he searched for the right instance to jump in. He remembered when he was younger, his older brothers and sisters would pile on a playground merry-go-round with the older boys turning it faster and faster and daring others to jump on the spinning ride. That took timing too, if one wanted to be spun to a drunken dizziness. Salvador watched Place and the bobbing became infectious.

"Take a step or two before the music ends," Rita warned and smiled at Mitch, who waited for her instructions.

Place committed himself to a step as he jumped forward. His timing was off, and Rita could see that immediately. "Stop and start over again," she instructed.

Salvador had followed Place's lead, and he stuttered forward with the music going north and his feet taking him south. "Tell

Salvador to stop too," Rita said and walked to her cassette player to start the song over. "Come here," she said as she positioned Salvador and Place on either side of her and held onto the hand of each. Bending her knees slightly and dipping her head and shoulders with the music, she let her body communicate the movements to Salvador and Place's bodies. At the precise musical moment, Rita stepped forward and pulled her two dance partners alongside her. Place and Salvador stumbled in tow like unschooled puppies who hadn't yet learned to walk on a leash. Halfway across the floor, Rita stopped and turned the two men around. Again they waited to catch the music at the right point. Rita moved forward and merged with the music. She continued to hold firmly to Salvador's and Place's hands, jerking back quickly to slow them down or squeezing their hands to bring them back up to the tempo.

Now it was Mitch's turn. Place was relieved and Salvador wiped his beading brow with the sleeve of his new shirt.

Facing them, Rita started backwards to show Mitch the pattern that her steps should take. Back and backwards toward the middle of the dance floor, Rita shuffled, her arms held in front of her as if an invisible partner led her through the music. She held her head at a slight upward angle, and her mouth was straight and serious. As she backed two steps and a shuffle at a time, Rita closed her eyes and went to the place where her dancing took her.

Repeatedly, Mitch, Place, and Salvador's feet stammered and sputtered as they tried to coordinate and acclimate their bodies to both motion and music. Repeatedly, three rigid and partnerless figures made solo sojourns as their tentative steps advanced them toward the middle of the dance floor and back. Repeatedly, Mitch, Place, and Salvador fell out of time with the music as the doldrums of their own rhythm left them bobbing and waiting to catch the next current of music. Repeatedly, like a confident coxswain, Rita urged on her stalled dancers by chanting: "step together, step together, step touch, step touch, step together, step together, step touch, step touch."

Rita watched carefully and patiently, studying form, function, and fluidity, and occasionally offering individualized instruction to her pupils. "Salvador, stand straighter. Tell him to stand straighter, Place. And you, Place, stop looking over at the crowd at the bar. They aren't watching you, anyway. Concentrate on your steps. Mitch, stop looking at your feet. You need to be able to make those moves without looking down." Rita allowed for a few more jagged passes and then decided to couple up Mitch and Place while she served as Salvador's partner.

Rita was emphatic in her lecture, pointing out the true difficulty it takes to achieve competent partner dancing. She focused on Place first, informing him of his responsibility in leading his partner. Positioning herself opposite Place and assuming the male lead position, Rita showed him how to guide his partner through inconspicuous, silent cues. She held her right hand firmly on Place's left shoulder blade as she led him backwards down the middle of the dance floor. She applied enough pressure with the cupped palm of her hand to signal to Place that they would shift to reverse. As their motion changed from backward to forward for Place, Rita talked him through the change of direction, explaining to him that his partner should always be held snugly in the rudder of his hand. Mitch and Salvador watched as the couple approached them. Halfway back to their starting point, Rita warned Place about their next move, two steps in place as the lead partner lifted her left hand high to twirl Place under her arm. It was a reach for Rita, but her sinewy and elastic body stretched long and lean as she guided Place through his spin and continued back toward the waiting students. In harmony, Mitch and Salvador breathed out appreciative oohs to show how impressed they were.

"Now, Mitch and Place, you partner up and I'll take Salvador," Rita instructed. She walked over to the small corner table and changed cassettes. "We'll go with the line of dance, because when you dance with the big kids you need to know the right direction so you don't get in anybody's way." She made a sweeping counterclockwise motion to remind her pupils of the pattern and direction of the dance floor. Rita waited for Place to translate to Salvador and when Place simply looked at him, pointed, and said, "Go that way," Rita proceeded to her next lesson. "As soon as this song ends, get ready to start with the next song. It's a two-step too. Now if you don't feel you started with the music, just count and listen for the rhythm to come around to where you can jump in."

Holding Mitch close to him, Place watched Salvador's back as he held Rita, and the four of them waited through the brief silence of the cassette and the muffled laughing and talking at the bar. The admonishing lyrics carried along by the confident, cantering tempo of "Jealous Heart" caught Mitch, Place, and Salvador off guard. Rita jerked Salvador toward her in an effort to catch up to the music. Salvador two-stepped onward as Mitch and Place jerked and jolted in their movements, trying to jump in anywhere in the music and not really listening as closely as they needed to.

"Stop!" Rita shouted from across the dance floor as her novice partner concentrated on keeping his steps to the paces of the music. When they had completed a circle, Rita stopped to help Mitch and Place get started. "Listen and count to the music," she said as she moved her body in place to the continuing song. Rita pointed to the cassette player and counted and clapped her hands in cadence to demonstrate to Mitch and Place the timing of the music.

"There!" Rita pointed out quickly. "And there! That's where you would come in. Do you hear that? It's important to recognize when you should start. And you don't necessarily need to begin when the song does. It takes couples a few bars to get on the floor anyway. And don't rush things. If you miss the start of the song, just wait." Rita rewound the cassette to play the same song again, explaining to the trio that it might help to first get familiar with dancing to the same tune for a while.

Salvador, intuiting the universal language and inflection of music, and slightly familiar with the Boot Hill Bar's dance floor and selected patrons, went with the tempo as the song started.

Rita held him with a firm submission that allowed her to be led around the dance floor while still feeling Salvador's body and subtle cues signaling directions, moves, and adjustments with his arms and hands. Carefully, intrinsically, intricately their bodies seemed to flow just as a skilled fiddler makes the bow skip and sway and in those motions makes music. So too, Salvador and Rita made music as together they accompanied notes and rhythms, absorbing them into the instruments that were their own bodies and displaying a coupled and kinesthetic interpretation through the patterns of two steps and a shuffle.

Mitch and Place waited. They didn't want to be influenced by Salvador and Rita's departure. As the rhythm came around, Place released the pressure of his cupped hand on Mitch's back and stepping toward her signaled that they too would embark on a circular journey counterclockwise. Place was cautious, and he concentrated hard on the movements in the music. Mitch stepped backwards while she studied her boots, often misstepping, stalling, and starting again.

"That's it, just start again," Rita urged while still dancing and studying the couple at the same time. "And Mitch, quit looking at your feet! It's your brain that's going to tell them where to go, not your eyes."

Mitch blushed as she looked at Place, whose serious expression showed that he was focused on the music.

After intermittent tips and suggestions and many "Jealous Hearts," Rita talked over the continuing cassette as she offered a closing lecture and further advice before ending the dance lesson. She was more philosophical in her approach now as she explained to her beginning dancers that partner dancing required a sense of intuition and communication. Yes, there were those slight, even somehow subconscious gestures that initiated an implied language of interaction, but to dance with a partner and know that language required a lot of time together at first. "You need to communicate with the language of your body when you're dancing. Help each other with the vocabulary of your movements," Rita concluded as she moved on to another point.

Mitch smiled to herself as she thought about her younger years of dressage training. Those movements too, between horse and rider were somehow communicated, and one led while the other responded. In competition when both horse and rider were interacting as only two living souls do when they spend enough time to recognize the patterns and rhythms of each other's organic and sensuous language and life, the dance could be enchanting to watch and experience. Mitch's skin twitched with excitement, and bashful goosebumps populated her arms, shoulders, and back, and she remembered that exquisite, perfect dance with a throwaway mare she had saved, succored, and trained. The day before her refined mare was to enter its first competition, Mitch rode her bareback over the hills behind her girlhood home and to the softly swirling stream where she baptized the horse Galatea in a formal and solemn ceremony. After the baptism, Mitch walked back to her home with her newly christened creation alongside her, and talking to her horse as if talking to a close friend.

Rita closed her lesson by talking about the postures in dancing, especially in a place like hers. Partner dancing, according to Rita, did many things. Partner dancing defined boundaries; it told others who belonged to whom, and it further established the unspoken norms of cowboy etiquette. Partners mostly dance only with each other, Rita philosophized, and if somebody else wants to dance with either one of them, they have to ask the other partner if they may. "So, Mitch," Rita pointed out, "if somebody wants to dance with your man, that somebody should ask you and not Place. And the same goes for you too, Place." Rita directed her colloquium toward Salvador and explained how his was a different situation. Salvador was more in unsettled territory when it came to partner dancing. He would have to find a partner and in a place like the Boot Hill Bar, that "partner" could be solicited by many suitors. "You just have to stay alert and polite," Rita offered to Salvador, who acknowledged her with a nodding head and knowing smile.

To conclude her presentation, Rita talked about attitude in dancing. It was important, for the woman especially, to dance with aloof and confident conviction. To achieve that, Rita asserted, the woman had to be a stoic dancer. She had to hold her head up with a straight line marking her mouth, not a curving smile or a toothy grin that gave away the true pleasure of dancing. The lady's left hand should be positioned softly on her man's right shoulder with fingers extended gracefully and touching, not splayed like a chicken's foot or clutching out of torrid desperation. Rita demonstrated, as she held her own head slightly upward, arm raised, and her hand gracefully extended like a ballerina, the seriousness of partner dancing. She explained, to Mitch more than to Place and Salvador, that as a dancing pair made the counterclockwise circle around the dance floor, those who were not dancing would be observing. It was to those observers that many messages were conveyed through the uplifted head, the straight statement of a mouth, and attitude of which Rita spoke. "When you're dancing with Place, Mitch," Rita started, "you need to show that that's your man. And that look should show that the two of you have been through a lot, good and bad, and that as you are on any night you're partner dancing, the two of you will stay together through more thick and thin if you need to. That says a lot for a couple, and people will understand that if they have even as much sense as a mule. Folks, at least around here, know not to sit in somebody else's saddle." Rita concluded her instruction and invited her students who were now guests to stay and practice what they had just learned.

The band set up their instruments on the little stage that jutted out from a dark wall like a pouting lip from a moody face. Mitch, Place, and Salvador claimed one of the many tables that lined the perimeter of the dance floor. A guitarist plunked at strings to test their sound and strength. Another man lovingly positioned his steel guitar toward the edge of the stage and off to one side. More couples arrived as dance time approached. Fewer men stood at the bar as those who dropped in for an after-work social left to prepare for another day of labor. On the replugged jukebox, a classic country song droned on as the words of a lonely singer floated out and away. Place watched as a solitary couple slow danced in their own corner to the singer's mournful lyrics. The male partner held his mate close and talked to her throughout their slow swaying. There was a low-glowing tightness that seemed to mark the couple with implicit confusion. Place watched them closely. He noticed the partly opened mouth of the young woman and thought about her slight smile, a sensuous, anticipatory smile that was repressed by ambivalent expectation.

The fiddler drew on his bow and tested the strings. He riffled through a few chords quickly and then practiced a sequence of exercises to limber up his fingers. "Testing, one, two, three. Testing, one, two, three. Hi y'all!" The lead guitarist's voice bassed out over the sound system. The drummer swept his drumsticks through a series of pattering movements. He shifted individual drums to the stand of space at the back of the small stage that allowed him and his talents to be more visually effective. A joking cocktail waitress delivered three ginger ales to Mitch, Place, and Salvador and told them she knew that they would be trouble tonight. The band members stood with their instruments ready, exchanged glances and nods, and began to play a properly respectful country song. The steel guitar moaned lonely sounds as the attentive musician tickled thick yet delicate sentimental notes from it that evaporated like frustrated sighs. Salvador sat quietly and watched the musicians comb and tease music from their instruments. Mitch watched as Rita, her body outlined by the silhouetted distance of low lights, welcomed arriving couples and proudly invited them to take a table. Place listened with sad admiration and silently craved a beer, more for the moment of the music than for the urge to be taken to a spot where he could forget.

Rita approached her students' table trailed by a younger woman who resembled her in many ways. She introduced her daughter to Mitch, Place, and Salvador and suggested that Salvador would have somebody safe to dance with. As the band prepared to begin their first set after playing an easy warm-up song, Rita's daughter walked over to the lead singer and whispered something to him. With quick, short steps that added a rhythmic attractiveness to the way she moved, Rita's younger image approached her new acquaintances and announced that the band would play some numbers they could two-step to. Without hesitating, she reached for Salvador's hand and invited him toward the dance floor. Feeling a little awkward, Mitch and Place followed cautiously.

Salvador and Rita's daughter caught the flow of music and smoothly floated into the line of dance as other couples bobbed and stepped along like vessels parading on a calm bay. Mitch and Place waited for couples to pass by them before they floated into the moving circle. Place was meticulous in making sure he held Mitch the way Rita had taught. As they waited for their timing before they would begin moving onward, a couple avoided sideswiping the waiting pair and two-stepped by them. Place and Mitch bobbed a little as they anticipated the moment they would shove off, and the moment finally came. They were in motion and their steps seemed to fit with the music. Place smiled widely and Mitch did too, her left hand anchoring into Place's shoulder. Together, they felt as if they were riding a bicycle for the first time. They shuffled by the band, and the lead singer nodded approvingly to Place. They sailed past tables of couples who were sitting this number out or simply watching the other dancers. They completed a full loop with pride and self-centered appreciation of their own partnered display, and they forgot about anybody else who might be dancing.

Place did not notice the pair in front of him until Mitch was backstepping into a larger man's backside. Both couples jerked to a stop, apologized, and the other twosome was on their way again. Place and Mitch stood motionless as they tried to make sense of their clumsy ways. Woodenly, they stepped off to the side to let others dance by. Place tried to align himself to Mitch's body, and when they both stepped forward they caromed off each other. In a stiff and ungainly way they pushed into the flow of dance traffic. Mitch took rapid steps backwards—certainly more than two steps and with hardly a shuffle. Place took little rapid running steps to catch up to her, but he kept yanking Mitch to a stop as he tried to remain faithful to the dance pattern. Their

174

movements were rigid and gauche and the music left them bumping, bouncing, and ricocheting to a rhythm that for them was now completely uncalibrated. Mitch and Place were relieved when the song ended and they were able to limp back to the safe harbor of their table. Across the floor, Salvador offered an awkward bow to his partner and thanked her for the dance.

"I can't believe I'm sweating this much," Place remarked as he pulled out a chair for Mitch to sit. "That's a lot of work."

"It is, especially when you're learning," Mitch agreed as she dabbed at the sweat on her forehead with a cocktail napkin.

Salvador, pleased with his ability to assimilate to the music and feeling confident because he liked the way his new clothes fit, smiled widely, almost foolishly, and with a radiating face said, "Es muy fun, huh?"

Place watched as the evening wore on. Drinks did not go wasted, but allowed others to put aside the things that might otherwise keep them from dancing in the first place. The line of dance did not seem to flow as smoothly as it had in the beginning. More raucous movements dominated the once synchronized dance floor. Bigger men, and by now more outgoing and gregarious men, hunched over shorter partners and improvised their dance steps. This interested Place. He assumed that all of the people in the Boot Hill Bar would naturally know how to dance to their music. He had thought it was a cultural inheritance, innate, or an archetype of motion and movement passed down through the cells, blood, and bones of the people he now studied. But the Boot Hill Bar showed Place something else. Even though he was a novice dancer and had only the Texas two-step in his repertoire of dancing, Place began to understand that he could fit into many cultures. Existence wasn't as narrow as he had previously felt it was. People didn't own their behavior, beliefs, or patterns of living simply by being born into them. A place like the Boot Hill Bar would welcome men like him and Salvador with few, if any, prerequisites. Comfortably, they could sit at the bar, have a drink, and discuss their day on the ranch and days to come. Place grew comfortable and his thinking expanded along with his psyche, knowing that the boundaries of his world had no specific locations, no determined areas or defined spaces. As an anthropologist gains entrée into an unknown world of knowing people, Place and Salvador, and even Mitch, were within and without. It was up to them, their effort, their interests.

Place watched as the big men danced freely, wildly—careening like dancing mavericks that dared to be corralled. Knees jerked high and elbows flapped and flailed. Legs kicked out in all directions and partners were flung around and about and reeled back in like yo-yos. Place was impressed by their size. It was their size that allowed them to be who they thought they were. Their size alone spoke many things to others. To other bigger men, size was a factor that could be challenged or respected, or challenged first and then respected. To some women, size was a protective and comforting thing, a tangible sign that a body was capable of trading labor for wages. To smaller men like Place, size could be a quick attribute with which to measure a man's disposition, because with size came force and big men often walked with a confident sense of force and puffed-up recognition. Place doodled on a cocktail napkin with a short, eraserless pencil that looked as if it had logged the scores of countless frames of bowling.

The fiddler pumped his instrument as he skillfully drew whining, screeching sounds that danced with the steel guitarist's unwinding and seductively sorrowful notes, his fingers gracefully skating along the strings. The thumping sounds from the drums and the sharp strumming of guitar strings followed the lead of the deeply modulated voice that expelled twangy, romantic lyrics of lost love for which only the singer was to be blamed. Looser, coarser dancers twirled and spun and swung arms and took impromptu steps as Place no longer looked but wrote on the cocktail napkin. Words were scratched out and more effective ones were put in their place. Arrows made curving points to show where lines needed to be rearranged, and alongside each line was a number to identify the order the lines should follow.

"What ya got there?" Mitch asked, sneaking a look like a school kid cheating on a test.

"A song," Place answered, sublimating an inclination to cover up the personal nature of writing and words. "Want to hear it?"

Before Place recited the lyrics he explained the three verses he had and pointed out what would be the chorus. He started slowly, as if reading poetry.

> I have always thought of myself as a big man
> But you know I get that stuff from a beer can.
> Honey I'm no bigger than I try to be
> Ever since the day you up and left me.

"That's the first verse," Place said. "Should I go on?"

"Well, of course," Mitch urged, interested by Place's poetic perceptions and social interpretation.

> Every twelve ounces made me feel bigger
> And knowin' you was waitin' made me feel slicker.
> But big and slick are only false feelings
> I need you to stop the hurt and start the healing.
>
> Yes, I sat around and took you for granted
> Not realizing this relationship was slanted
> So please come back and I'll tell you what I'm about
> Because I intend to straighten that slant out.

"Honey, that's good!" Mitch marveled. "When did you write that?"

"Just now," Place answered, a little surprised that Mitch actually thought his song was good. "Want to hear the chorus?"

Place started from the beginning again and after the first verse he threw in the chorus.

> So what I get from my drinkin'
> And what your leavin' brang me to thinkin'
> Is that I'm only a big man
> With you by my side instead of a beer can.

"It's called 'Big Man,' " Place said, not waiting for the question and feeling pleased that his song made sense to him. He liked it, even if it didn't have music yet.

"Well, you're catching on to the ways of this arena," Mitch joked. "We can get you more familiar with this culture by getting you home and to sleep so you can work a ranch tomorrow," she added to indicate that perhaps it was time to end the evening, especially as a louder and rowdier crowd had begun to infiltrate all corners of the dance floor and bar.

Silent from the experience of the evening, the emotion of Salvador's birthday, and the exhaustion that accompanies learning and practice, Mitch, Place, and Salvador moved along dark roads as the headlights of the pickup stabbed a lighted path into the black scenery that revealed little.

Turning the pickup off Sweet Wine Road and into StarRidge Ranch, Mitch whispered slowly and squinted into the darkness as she forced her eyes to focus. The pickup idled quietly as Mitch looked past Place and Salvador. "Ah, shit!" she uttered softly.

Off to the side, to their right and tucked alongside the milk barn apartment, sat Jacqueline and Mickey's conspicuous truck.

Jacqueline and Mickey's arrival surprised Mitch in many ways. Yes, it was unexpected—something that at first perturbed Mitch more than it bothered Place and Salvador, who had separately decided to work together in safe silence regardless of the demands—but Mitch was also caught off guard by the company the Kittles had brought along with them to live on the ranch.

First, there was the old paint cayuse, Duchess, a black-and-white splattered mare that had seen decades of riders and miles of trails and was now, in her senescent stage, facing the tribulations brought on by living too long. Duchess was Jacqueline's first horse from a time when she was a younger, more exuberant woman. When Mitch first set eyes on the decaying pony she wondered why the Kittles had even bothered to transport the animal to its new rest home at StarRidge Ranch. Duchess seemed long overdue to be packaged neatly and efficiently as Rosa and Coquette's food. Once at the ranch, Duchess was given her own private accommodations, a corral closest to Jacqueline and Mickey's milk barn apartment.

Duchess's bloom had long since abandoned her now cadaverous body, and her hide was splotchy with bald patches where hair refused to grow. Her sides were sunken, not from malnour-ishment—Mitch could see that, even if she did suspect underfeeding—but from years of gravity that tugged at the horse's once straight spine that was gerontologically swayed and a meager appetite brought on by boredom when one lives longer than even God may have intended. Her hip bones protruded, pointing outward against skin that seemed to hang and drawing her hide taut over a shrinking frame. Her body appeared dented like a well-used tube of glue. Her mane was mangy now, no longer possessing the full and long curtain of hair that had once draped her neck. Her forelock was completely gone. Her hoofs were free of the weight of horseshoes because there was no need for her to be shod, but Jacqueline had made sure that the horse's hoofs were regularly trimmed and well-cared for. The mare's teeth were tentative ones now, with her grinders worn close to the gum line; she was on a steady diet of soft, nourishing feed.

Mitch could see as Jacqueline stroked her old friend that the horse's eyes were dull; there was little life left in them. But it was-n't Duchess that Mitch observed as Jacqueline scratched her horse's neck and held her muzzle gently.

Jacqueline seemed to truly care for Duchess. She was devot-ed to the horse, and in the week since the Kittles had moved on the ranch permanently it was clear that only Jacqueline would feed this dying horse. Even when Mitch had offered to take care of Duchess to free Jacqueline up so she might be able to tend to less mundane chores and business, Jacqueline had declined the offer. Mitch noticed too that Jacqueline was proud of Duchess, and she admired the fact that the horse was meaningful enough to keep alive and be allowed to finish her days in dignity in a bucol-ic pasture on StarRidge Ranch. The halcyon care served as a tranquilizer for the feeble horse, and as a side effect medicated the scowling surliness that had been Jacqueline's primary symptoms.

Duchess's presence seemed to somehow draw Mitch closer to Jacqueline. During free moments of a busy work day, Mitch and Jacqueline would lean against a fence or sit on a deck and talk about the aging animal, with those conversations often drifting off into other areas concerning the ranch, the community, and the county.

Mickey's new pet was a gigantic, powerful Clydesdale named Bunny. When Bunny arrived two days after the Kittles had settled in, Mitch, Place, Salvador, Jacqueline, and Mickey watched as the professional transporters eased the huge horse out of a long slip of a trailer. Slowly they backed the behemoth from the trailer and down a wide, slight, short ramp. The two handlers worked like tugboats carefully and methodically pushing a large vessel out to sea. With each deliberate backward step, the handlers leaned away from Bunny, surveying the open ocean of land behind and around him. Once Bunny hit the dry dock of solid earth, he craned his neck, reaching high and somewhat nervously scanning the new environment before and around him. His ponderous steps sent radiating waves that rumbled and vibrated through the feet and upward to those who looked on. He was fully developed, and his body blossomed with massive muscles. Bunny's high, straight back, wide hips, and loglike legs were punctuated by big, brawny bones. The unique full feathers on his lower legs hung loosely and swayed like hula skirts as he strode alert but relaxed toward his new pasture. He was oddly controlled by only a lead rope attached to a halter that looked like a string compared to the vastness of the animal. Holding the lead rope cautiously, Mickey walked carefully beside Bunny, the handlers on the opposite side guiding him delicately with outstretched arms. Bunny drifted compliantly into the harbor of his new home. Easy, swaggering steps affected cut and plated muscles that armored the draft horse's body, which shifted and slid slickly with each movement.

Bunny was a brontosaurus of a horse whose capable musculature interested Mickey. His goal was to someday hitch the workhorse up to a plow to work the pastures as had been done a century earlier. Reaching easily over the fence, Bunny sucked up a whole carrot from Mickey's hand and chewed it with the same nonchalant pace that his movements indicated.

Although Mitch found both new tenants to be peculiar choices for the Kittles to have, she was also slightly impressed with the concern that Mickey and Jacqueline showed for Duchess and Bunny. This made Mitch feel a little foolish, and she wondered why she hadn't realized months earlier that much of what she disliked about the Kittles, and had experienced because of them, may have been due to the tremendous strain they had been under. After all, it was Mitch who once tried to explain to Place that StarRidge Ranch was a tremendous responsibility with many demands. Mitch herself had told Place that should they some day own their own StarRidge Ranch, she would not want a spread even half that size. Place had agreed, along with Salvador, that a property the size of this ranch was simply too much work with little satisfaction in return. As she watched Jacqueline one morning lovingly feeding her first Duchess, Mitch scolded herself for not being more understanding and tolerant of the Kittles. She questioned her ability, honed by her professional training but now left to grow dull with little verbal sparring to keep her in disputative shape, and wondered if for some self-centered reason she was slipping when it came to reading and knowing people, clients, criminals, and critters and the motivations that drove them. In her pensive moment, Mitch thought that she had perhaps been too quick to judge what she and Place had experienced with the limitations of fleeting events and occurrences. She had taken such pride in being compassionate and fair-minded—sometimes to a fault. Now she felt ashamed and admonished herself for forgetting one of the vital tenets of introductory law. Mitch had fallen into the stifling quicksand of making murky assumptions.

Place, however, was not impressed. If anything, he was gleefully, almost arrogantly suspicious, and he advanced his position in elaborate detail as he tried one night to persuade Mitch that the Duchesses and Bunnies of the world were distractions for deeper, more dysfunctional attributes. Many families had those distractions; they made things appear normal in an abnormal world. They were necessary links in the social chain of human interaction and discourse. Those distractions came in many, often subtle, forms. Going to church was one. Obvious displays of volunteerism and community service were another. Social recognition—an effective diversion for those *other* things that were happening behind the barn, Place theorized. "I think the mind does that," he stated matter-of-factly, "as a way for us to convince ourselves that we are really okay as people, even though we are, for the most part, contradictory and hypocritical animals." To show how credible he was, he added: "I do it all the time. We both know I have a lot to resolve with myself."

There was too much charm in what was developing and how it was developing, Place argued. The actions were too pastoral, too affected, and he wondered who it was that the Kittles might be trying to impress. Certainly, he propounded, it couldn't be him and Mitch. Also, Place suggested, as he pointed a knowing finger at Mitch while she sat up in bed listening to her postulating husband as he paced back and forth, what had been the Kittles', especially Jacqueline's, reaction to the murdered ducks? What kind of sympathy had they shown after Mitch pointed out the dried blood on the pipe fencing and the embedded feathers that lay scattered in the dirt? Pounding a fist into a palm he shouted dramatically, "Nothing! No reaction! Nada." Now lowering his voice almost to a whisper and showing that he had paid close attention on those now faraway nights when Mitch had asked him to critique her closing arguments, judging for artistic performance as well as content, Place ingratiated himself by elaborating on his own ignorance, his own confusion, which really was a seductive move that indicated he wasn't buying any of it.

"Ms. Stanton," he said formally, "wouldn't someone who is truly concerned about life, someone who truly cares about the welfare of all creatures, especially when you own those creatures, when those creatures who are your very subjects, under your care, and it's faith and trust that causes them to care—wouldn't that person show a little more emotion and concern for what happened to those flightless, helpless ducks, ducks as capable as a dodo bird, ducks bound to the ground and restricted in their survival like immigrants with their own foreign language, than what you yourself admit was a dismissing reaction on the part of Jacqueline Kittle?"

Mitch was taken by the argument. Her skin itched and seemed to undulate like the slow movements of an exploring snake, and a warm, comforting glow soothed her stomach as it turned into a blue flame that reached for her heart. She sat straighter and prepared her statement, grateful for the rational jousting Place had incited in her. She dissected his argument; she charitably acknowledged the strong points of his position; she formulated careful equations with ideas, assumptions, and values. She explained to her husband that there were very few common denominators that could be clearly factored in, and finally she showed Place how in the mathematics of language and thought, "You're always going to have that annoying remainder of one. It doesn't fit neatly, Mr. Moreno. Not at all. Not at all."

* * *

In the tentative early spring days, the two owners and the three ranch hands worked side by side reviving the fences, pastures, sheds, and other structures of the ranch from the long, wet winter. In the evenings Mitch and Jacqueline visited with Duchess and talked informally and even amiably about things each would like to do with various aspects of their lives. In the calming quiet that seemed to emanate from Duchess's aura, the two women of the ranch shared more and more with one another.

Mickey too appeared to be more settled, and each afternoon when the work day was declared over he visited Bunny, often combing the burrs and twigs from the long, white feathers on his legs and feeding him carrots as a possessed gambler feeds a slot machine.

Salvador had wondered one early morning before beginning another day of work if the Kittles' new animals were having a therapeutic effect on them. From the first day they had moved in, the Kittles no longer exuded such a strict sense of urgency or desperation. Duchess's aged wisdom and Bunny's complacent presence were like doses of comforting sedatives, and more work was accomplished with less stress now that Jacqueline and

Mickey could benefit from the calming vibrations of their animals. Surveying the couple from a safe distance, Salvador reminded Mitch and Place how important it was to have someone or something to care for. There was a sense of humble pride in knowing that one animal, whether a biped or quadruped, had another to rely on, to care for, to cry to, and to comfort.

Standing short, bent, and haggard, Duchess displayed a sense of patient fortitude and faith. She was an example of constancy and a chamomile of an animal. Indirectly she reminded those who cared for her that long-range goals were vital to doing and being. Bunny, standing tall, straight, and vigorous, foretold of promise in what the future could bring, and residually his presence meant effort and reward. He was an animal that represented potential and possibility.

As the two new members of StarRidge Ranch modestly assumed center stage and Jacqueline and Mickey's focused attention, the calves, burros, and other horses paid homage to Duchess's fortitude and Bunny's size. Calves bellowed in a chorusing tribute, burros blasted trumpets of praise, and gregarious horses whinnied in royal pride at the arrival of their new ranch mates.

The spring days became longer and StarRidge Ranch grew greener. White fences sparkled brightly, announcing who belonged where and who owned what. From the balance that Duchess and Bunny brought to the ranch and especially to the Kittles, the scales of sensibility and interaction evened out more reasonably than they ever had since the day the sixty-acre spread had oozed into the lives of Mitch, Place, Jacqueline, Mickey, and Salvador.

The three men stood clear as the third and final pine tree came crashing to the ground. Seismic vibrations shook the earth around the fallen trees, and shards of shattered branches cracked, snapped, and burst in explosions of long life cut dead by the unfeeling bite of Mickey's chain saw with its long, phallic blade. Flat-topped stumps sat like warts, skinned blemishes that would remain rooted in the body of StarRidge Ranch. As soon as the earth settled and it was clearly safe to move on, Place and Salvador attacked the trees with hand saws and pruning shears, amputating dying limbs from their corpses. A high pile of entangled branches grew as the trees were turned into tapered logs.

Bunny stood in workmanlike devotion as he waited for Mickey and Salvador to adjust the choker of chain to one of the trees. Place held Bunny's harness loosely. He looked closely into the enormous horse's eyes and could see a distorted reflection of himself. Bunny stared back knowingly. Mickey checked the chains that ran on either side of Bunny, and once he was sure the log was secure, he clicked softly with his tongue pressed against the roof of his mouth. Click, click, click and slowly, Bunny marched forward, dragging the lifeless log to an open space on the ranch. A skid road beveled into the earth as the last log was dragged to where Place and Salvador would begin incremental cuts of rounds that would later be split into fireplace-ready wedges.

Cutting logs would have to wait, however, and as Place and Salvador walked away from the death camp of dead wood, Mickey inspected Salvador's round help house.

The plans were elaborate. Mickey spelled out carefully to Place as he translated to Salvador how the squat house would be transformed into a functional unit, complete with its own toilet and a new roof. Windows would have new panes of glass; the floors would be linoleumed and carpeted; walls would be painted and bordered "in farm colors" as Mickey explained, and new tenants would be able to rent this Cinderella of a house. Salvador, who was granted an extended but vague stay of employment by the Kittles, would be moved to a stall in the stall barn. His outhouse would follow him as they repositioned it closer to the backside of the barn.

Mickey was an artisan. Place and Salvador stood like eager apprentices while Mickey worked out problems on plywood with a broad, flat pencil. Salvador was impressed as Mickey circled the answer to an algebraic or geometric problem and then declared to himself that they would need this many two-by-fours, and that many sheets of sheetrock. From an ancient Aztec inheritance, Salvador explained to Place what and how Mickey was calculating. Mickey estimated the amount of linoleum and carpet that would be sufficient. They climbed to the top of the house, and Mickey figured out how many rolls of tarpaper and bales of shingles would patch up the perforated roof. He determined what types of nails would bring the little house into the current century. With his hammer, Mickey knocked on various parts of bearing walls, testing for stoutness and stability. He listened carefully, lightly tapping, reaching high and low—his hammer serving as a stethoscope and his diagnosis confirming what he suspected. They would proceed immediately with surgical diligence and precision.

Almost daily, Jacqueline and Mitch visited hardware stores, furniture lobbies, and specialty shops as they looked for just the right porcelain knobs, brass fixtures, appropriate doors, thick enough carpet, and a linoleum pattern that was ranch ready. Jacqueline ran her fingers and thumb over material that could be cut and sewn into tasteful curtains. Together, they judged various designs of wallpaper. At a paint store, Jacqueline held a swatch of curtain material against a panel of various colors. She asked Mitch for her opinion, and gratefully yet carefully, Mitch offered her point of view, always reminding herself to measure her words, to restrict a true judgment, deferring to Jacqueline the private pleasure of being the one who really knew how to appoint and furnish her own homes.

Over fluffy croissants and fancy, foamy coffee served in petite cups, Jacqueline and Mitch sat at an umbrellaed table in front of a fashionable European-style bakery. Men with sweaters draping their shoulders and women wearing riding boots sat at their own tables talking about wine, polo, and good years. Blondes with big teeth laughed indifferently, and men whose muscles were developed from "working out" rather than "working at" gave serious consideration to a menu that listed flavors and blends of chic coffees. Jacqueline explained in architectural detail the plans she had for StarRidge Ranch. The Kittles would bring two trailers onto the property— one was really a mid-sized mobile home—and they would situate them behind the remodeled help house. Mickey's skills in eclectic plumbing would allow him, with the help of Salvador and Place, to tap the new dwelling's plumbing into the aged septic system of the remodeled help house. More tenants—human ones—would move in to help offset the ranch mortgage by renting the trailers. A well-written ad using phrases like "country charm" and "quiet living" would bring them in.

Mitch shrank as she listened, trying to hide her shock at the news of what she considered would develop into StarRidge Mobile Home Park. She tried to recall what she knew about landlord and tenant law. More vital to her concerns and to those who presently lived on the ranch, Mitch wondered about health codes, fire codes, building codes; a collection of codes and county regulations snapped in front of her as she mentally listed the possibilities and improbabilities. Jacqueline casually and with familiarity raised her hand to summon a garçon, and as he returned with another dainty cup of creamed coffee with chocolate shavings slowly disappearing in it, she worked out the figures for Mitch to show how the trailer park business could be as lucrative as the horse business.

Mentally Mitch evaluated the backward progression of StarRidge Ranch as she explained to Place and Salvador what would be occurring in the near future and how the living arrangements would be altered.

Place maintained his superior smugness about the Kittles, wearing an I-told-you-so expression on his face and commenting, "Yeah, they're going to alter this place like a bad plastic surgeon alters an already fine face."

Salvador now privately hated the Kittles and he searched his memory to see if he had ever hated anyone in his life before. He knew that his growing rage was wasted energy. Living in the barn was only temporary, and really all life was, but he interjected to ask, "¿Cómo voy a comer?" Then he answered his own question about how he would eat with an explanation of how he could not cook in the barn: "No puedo cocinar en el barn. ¿Qué creen ellos?" And again he answered his own question, this one about what the Kittles could be thinking: "Creen que soy como un burro. ¡No! Ni los burros ni los otros animales se tratan así." He choked on his last words as the emotion constricted his throat and he shook his head as he stared over at where his new home would be.

"Poco a poco," Mitch counseled as she stared at the two men. "I'll talk to both of those freaks and see if we can work something out. For now, let's just proceed with their game plan and not try to change anything. What they don't know is that we'll be calling the plays soon."

Place started early on the help house, stripping it of dead and decaying material. He peeled the weather-worn shingles from the roof as if peeling skin from a sunburned body, and with the spring breeze fanning him, he enjoyed the life of a carpenter. It was a constructive life. It was a productive life. He, with Mickey's guidance and Salvador's assistance—once the animals were fed and cared for—could help to resurrect the short shack of a house. It would be a new life, a new beginning, building permits notwithstanding, and to bring life to something that was dying was rewarding.

Mickey assigned specific hammers and tape measures to both Place and Salvador and told them to keep them. Occasionally he would gift them with various things like a nail bag or utility belt to hold various tools. Each morning, Place and Salvador cinched their tool belts with deliberate confidence. They liked the feel of the weight that hugged their waists—holstered tools that they knew how to use or were learning about, and from that knowledge a strange sense of assured power. They each earned a personal saw, and Place and Salvador laughed as they joked about the superior dientes or teeth of their respective new tools.

One day after many hours of wrenching clinging, screaming nails from their once secure strongholds and rebuilding walls and window joists, Mickey approached the deck of the ranch house where Place and Salvador sat. Casually, he rewarded each man with a level. Place stood and inspected the instrument and thanked Mickey. Oddly, Place liked Mickey. He admired him. He relented to the ensnaring force of knowledge as he had in college when professors offered their regal, doubtless intelligence and persuasive suggestions. Salvador placed the level on the picnic table and looked carefully as one would look through a microscope or telescope. A bubble of fluid leaned dramatically to the leftmost end of the little glass cylinder. He nodded his head approvingly as Place caressed his new tool and found an appropriate home for it in his utility belt. He loved his tools, especially because they came from Mickey, the maestro who could master angles, see designs where none existed, and bring life to empty spaces. Tools from Mickey were merit badges, and in his enthusiasm and new learning, Place wanted more.

Inside the help house, Place and Salvador banged in nails as the walls were converted to an unpainted yet brighter and less blemished complexion. They measured and cut rectangles of plywood to fit flush with other sheets of wood that gave the walls new skin. They hardly spoke as music from a dilapidated radio groaned out sad songs in Spanish. Steadily, they raced the sun to see if they could finish the living room walls and move on to another room of the house the next day, each day measuring their success and each day bringing more learning.

Mickey, who grew confident in Place and Salvador's ability to follow instructions and bored with his own knowledge and expertise, concentrated on Bunny, training him more and more every day as he prepared him to pull things from a collar, yoke, and special harness. It was a queer and contrasting sight to watch Mickey, his body thin but not lanky, order and command Bunny to perform various tasks like backing up to a waiting plow or moving forward at a certain pace. Mickey stroked his working horse and praised him, and he was pleased.

For the first time, StarRidge Ranch was satisfying. Jacqueline and Mitch began to strip down much of the inside of the ranch house in preparation for the next phase of remodeling. The help house waited patiently for yellows and light blues and bordered windows of white to bring it to respectability. Place and Salvador inspected the bristles of their new paint brushes and squeezed the plushness of thick paint rollers, and as soon as Mickey had finished up the house by delicately tapping in the molding and fitting in the new doors, they would be let loose with brushes, rollers, buckets, pans, and paint.

Mickey sat regally atop Bunny, having discovered a special saddle that was big enough and girth extenders that were long enough to cover the table top of the horse's back and circumnavigate the hull of his body. He rode like Hannibal on his elephantine horse and inspected the land—*his* land—StarRidge Ranch. The other animals of the ranch watched carefully, grateful that the fences held them in and huge Bunny out. His size was unintentionally ominous, and his thunderous hooves pounded announcements of his and Mickey's arrival. The now neglected horses, who had originally come to the ranch as the jewels of Jacqueline and Mickey, watched him stride by, and they kept their distance, usually remaining in the middle of a pasture rather than curiously hugging the fences and reaching over sociably. The burros paced nervously, careful to mind their ways, and the growing calves chewed blankly as they watched master and animal glide by as if in a processional.

Only Joker brayed mockingly every time man and horse rode by, and Bunny would shake his head in annoyance, pick up his tempo to trot away, and slowly settle down to the soothing therapy of Mickey's voice and calming caresses. Mickey, equally vexed by Joker's taunting and harsh hollers, reprimanded the burro from eighteen hands high and assuaged Bunny's rattled nerves that Joker agitated into electric jumpiness.

On a dusky, dying evening, Mickey approached Joker, halter in hand, and prepared to move him to a corral that was closer to the stall barn yet out of the path of his daily rides with Bunny. He reached out slowly, murmuring "Whoa, Joker. Whoa, boy." As he raised the halter to capture the burro's head, Joker reared back and snorted a warning. Mickey, impatient and cursing Jacqueline for keeping her useless burros, stepped closer, crouching as if to make himself smaller and therefore less visible. Joker snorted menacingly; he warned Mickey as he had warned him each day he rode by, and he stepped backwards with each of Mickey's forward steps—an odd dance between two unwilling partners. Standing frozen, like the still lives that waited in Miwok Creek for the night to release them, Joker eyed Mickey as he continued to approach.

Mickey snapped the halter over the unmoving burro and in a lightning movement Joker swung his head fiercely, crashing flatly into Mickey's face and knocking him to the ground. Taking the proud prances of a bull that has confused a matador, Joker circled wide as Mickey cupped his nose and attempted to stop the flow that colored his face like the crimson streak left by the departing sun. Joker snorted long, slow expulsions of air; his head dipped but his eyes watched Mickey.

* * *

"You guys did a good job," Jacqueline marveled as she inspected the inside of the remodeled house while Place and Salvador scrapped out material and tools and prepared to wash up. "We can start putting the wallpaper and curtains up tomorrow."

The slow groan and clicking rattles of the pipes released frustrated air as Place slowly turned the spigot behind the help house. Salvador carefully poured turpentine into Place's cupped hands as he rinsed paint from them. In the distance, the cows from Sweet Milk Dairy mooed softly, calling to calves that had never suckled from their mothers' nourishment. In the ranch house, Mitch turned on the dance music as she prepared dinner, and moving backwards, she two-stepped into the kitchen.

In the farthest corral, the one closest to Miwok Creek, a river of angry red blood poured a tributary under the fence and toward the deadening silence that shrouded the still waterway. Joker lay dying, his mouth forming a silent, shocked rictus, the decibels of past brays now floating to heaven. His empty eyes dulled like setting winter suns, while swirls of dusty dirt sputtered as his nostrils flared in weakening gasps.

Place wavered, and he felt as if he would faint when Mickey approached him and Salvador and offhandedly told them to bury Joker.

"He's dead," Mickey said simply as he walked away, his face cracked and creased with dry blood. He held his hunting rifle firmly, the blue veins in his arm rigid and pumping life into a solid grip. Taking pounding steps that mimicked Bunny's, he retreated to his milk barn apartment.

The can of turpentine emptied into the ground, slowly oozing and mixing with the spigot that remained on, but now alone.

Place breathed hard, trying to catch his breath after running to Joker's corral. His face was contorted with a bizarre expression, the muscles in his cheeks twisting a corner of his mouth upward, and his forehead squeezed into disbelieving ridges. Salvador, accustomed to witnessing various forms of death, inured now to what life could mean, rushed to the ranch house to notify Mitch before they both ran out to the reddening corral.

Uselessly, Place stroked the dead burro as he knelt close to him. He choked out words that now meant nothing. He unconsciously traced the God-given cross, running his hand up and across the animal's back.

Salvador walked away quietly, only inspecting the burro momentarily, seemingly paying no attention nor tribute to what was now becoming a carcass.

Mitch knelt beside her sobbing husband. She slowly wavered back and forth, mourning silently but tearlessly. With one hand, she worked Place's neck with a soothing massage. With the other, she closed the lids over eyes that had seen more than they had ever revealed.

Salvador slid through the gate, leaned two shovels against the fence, and with his new saw began to cut through the side of the corral that bordered Miwok Creek. He breathed evenly with each stroke of his saw, and he continued unfazed as the saw jerked and cut through wire, downward, diligently downward, until he cut into the earth of StarRidge Ranch. Without looking back or cleaning the dirt and metal shavings from his saw, he measured out a panel wide enough to drag the burro through, and again cut downward into the fence until the ground signaled for him to stop.

"Plácido," he whispered like a mother gently waking her son, "tenemos que enterrar este pobre animal. Ayúdame, hombre, por favor." His voice was distant and detached; it was in another country. Looking around as if surprised to find himself where he was, Place looked at Salvador questioningly. His eyes showed that he didn't understand; life made him ignorant, but death made him dumb. Salvador tore away the section of sawed fencing as Mitch slowly walked back to the ranch house.

In the dark density of Miwok Creek, Salvador worked steadily. Each time the blade of the shovel dug into the soft earth it emerged with a full load of rich, black dirt—healthy and alive dirt—and it smelled sweet to Salvador. He first marked a rectangular perimeter of a grave and then started to hollow out the ground until he was satisfied that he had a proper burial site for Joker.

Without uttering a sound, and now deadly alive from the shock, Place began digging catatonically alongside his friend. Their eyes adjusted to the nightscape that consumed them as their bodies sank into the growing hole. Those animals that would be hunting for their food stayed hidden or hunted elsewhere. In the quiet and respectful silence, the earth announced echoes of clomping hoof steps.

Chains muffled a rattled sound as if they were being dragged by vengeful ghosts. The gate to Joker's corral squeaked open, and Mitch whispered clicking sounds as she led Bunny inside. The harness and yoke were affixed in the same manner in which he had dragged logs, and a large tarp straddled his back. Mitch continued to calm Bunny as he reacted nervously to the smell of blood, his lips flapping momentarily as he expelled a restive purr. She snapped a lead rope to his halter and tied him to a solid fence post. She watched for a few moments to see if he would accept his new position. Uncannily, Bunny seemed to sense the urgency of the moment; he cooperated by standing in the still darkness that hushed all movement.

Looking up, Salvador nodded approvingly and continued to dig. The two men emerged from the dark hole and clairvoyantly, Salvador took the tarp from Bunny's back. He unfolded it and tucked an edge of it carefully along and as close to Joker's body as he could. He whispered sharply to Place, almost scolding him, and urged him to help. Mitch walked quickly to Joker's shoulders and straddling them as Salvador pushed on the front portion of his body, she grabbed his front legs, pointing them toward the night sky and twirling stars. From her back pocket, she pulled a piggin string, one normally used in calf roping, and as if she was being timed she wrapped the string securely around the lower portion of his legs. She walked to the other end of the supple animal as Salvador pivoted on his knees and pushed against the side of the burro's rear, and again she secured another string to bind his rear legs. Mitch and Salvador struggled to slide the tarp under Joker's warm form. They swung his bound legs to one side and they strained as they pulled hard on the tarp. In his frustration,

Salvador wanted to yell at Place, who pulled unnoticeably, life-lessly, and was really only in the way. They were ancient Egyptians building a dead pyramid. Blood mixed with the dirt and formed a sodden quagmire of slippery pools. Finally securing the tarp from the withers to the flank, they swathed Joker tightly.

Mitch untied Bunny from the post and walked him through the section of cut-out fence and just outside it. Salvador stretched the chains straight toward Joker's body. With fluttering fingers, he motioned toward Mitch to back the workhorse up and occa-sionally looked toward Place, who stood mute, seemingly retarded. Blood and dirt caked Salvador's hands as he dug into the ground under Joker's backside. When he tucked both chains as far under as he could, he hissed urgently to Place to grab the burro's front legs while he grabbed the back ones. Together, they swung the animal toward the chains. With hands like desperate gophers, Salvador dug under the barrel of Joker's body and groped blindly for the hard coolness of the chains. He grunted in measured thrusts as he pulled on one chain and then the other. The tarp crumpled as Salvador secured the bolts to links of the chains, and standing straight with his boots, pants, T-shirt and arms plastered with bloody mud, he shook his head slowly as his desperate eyes met Mitch's. He panted heavily, his shoulders shrugging upward and his body reacting to regain the oxygen he had lost from working, wondering, and wanting to be somewhere else. Flicking his hands toward Mitch, he signaled for her to put Bunny's horsepower in motion.

Slowly, in the dark desperation of Miwok Creek, Mitch coaxed the willing horse on. She started out straight for the deep grave, and as she neared the berm of dirt that bordered it, she pushed the huge horse from the hole, angling it away. Mitch clicked gently with her tongue. Salvador watched as Joker's body twisted and turned from the initial movement, and slowly, slow-ly his body inched closer to his final home.

The thud of his dead weight and the crunch of bones broke the sweet, musty silence as Mitch and Salvador pushed Joker into the grave. Place stood staring at the hole with its eternal occupant. Grabbing the shovels, Salvador handed one to Place, look-ing closely into his eyes, measuring responsiveness, looking for life, and finding little of either. After a shovelful of dirt, Mitch walked close to the grave, squatted toward it and tossed in a car-rot. The two men covered the hole while Mitch quietly returned Bunny to his pasture.

Walking toward the ranch house, Place, Salvador, and Mitch did not speak. The ranch road dipped slightly and because of gravity they all picked up the pace. But Place walked more defi-antly, more vengefully with each step and each thought, urged onward now by more than just the declivity of the road, and grasping the shovel like a man holding on to a club, his walk broke into a clipping trot.

He was quick, and when Mitch and Salvador reacted they dropped the saw and shovel and ran after Place. Salvador reached for the shovel rather than for the man who intended to use it for an unintended purpose, and Mitch tried to wrap her arms around Place's body. They scuffled for moments as the three of them tumbled to the hard dirt road. Salvador grabbed at Place's legs and Mitch put all of her weight on him, pinning him to the ground.

"Honey! Place! Wait—" she started as she struggled to com-municate some common sense to him. "Place, no! Place, wait!"

Crying brokenly and hating the cruelty that God allowed, Place squirmed and twisted and sputtered, "I want revenge!" And then as if needing to make it clear to Salvador, "¡Yo quiero mi venganza!" He crawled along the ground scratching at the dirt to break free from both his wife and his best friend. All of the defeats in his life flashed before him, fanning the hot lights of bitterness and the acidulous anger that he could never quite extinguish.

In soothing, medicated, and mantric tones, Mitch repeated, "Place, we're leaving. Place, we're leaving tonight, right now. Now let's go, honey. Come on, sweetheart. We're leaving, Place. We're leaving the ranch."

A dull night light flickered in the upper floor of the Kittles' milkbarn apartment, and somewhere they cut into thick slabs of prime rib and washed it down with rich bold red wine. From the ranch house a gleaming glow radiated, and it looked as if every light was on. All of the faucets from the kitchen sink to the bathtub roared freely with flowing water, stoppers and rags punched in securely to ensure that they would fill and then overflow. Off to one side and blocked by the brightness spraying from the ranch house, a slowly idling engine putted and a truck waited patiently. In the darkness of StarRidge Ranch, in the peacefulness of the community around Sweet Wine Road, Mitch and Salvador walked Place toward their silent brown truck, each of them holding firmly to his upper arms. Glimmering red dots of lights signaled to them from the idling truck next to theirs, and it sat loaded with all of the belongings that Mitch and Place had moved to the ranch.

Paul Legarratta and his son sat waiting in their truck.

Mitch and Salvador eased Place into the little pickup. Salvador studied Place closely for a moment and then quickly ran to his stall barn room.

"You okay, Mitchy?" Legarratta asked seriously, occasionally looking toward the milk barn apartment and the entrance to the ranch while his son held a rifle loosely between his legs.

"Yeah, Pauly," Mitch said as she wiped her sniffling nose and drew in a deep and exasperated breath. "We're okay. We're going to be okay, Pauly."

"The cottage will be ready for you, Mitchy, when you get there. It'll be tight with the three of you and your animals, but that's the best I can do," Legarrata said assuredly and then as if apologizing. Wanting to comfort Mitch and knowing he didn't need to, Legarrata pushed on the clutch, patted Mitch's arm gently, shifted the truck into gear, and said, "Remember, you owe me one, Mitchy."

Mitch smiled shyly, and almost embarrassed, she walked toward the cab of her truck. In the back, Rosa and Coquette stood excited and alert, poking their heads from each side. Salvador came running toward the truck, clumsily holding a box of assorted clothing in one hand and clutching Gatita in the other. Place was wedged in between Mitch and Salvador, who draped an arm around Place as if to hold him up and back.

Michelle Stanton held the bottom of the steering wheel loosely and the dingy brown truck seemed to float on the dirt and gravel entrance of StarRidge Ranch. As they left the ranch, Salvador waved to the little help house. They drove on Sweet Wine Road into the darkness that would soon blaze with life-giving sunlight. The open land lay still, almost dead. Long streaks from leaning trees sent out darker points of murky and sullen shadows. Deeper into the undulating valleys, past productive farms and ranches, leaving orderly orchards and vineyards behind, and onward to where the horizon crashes with consistent, rhythmic, pounding waves, the weathered truck chugged along.

Salvador watched carefully, his eyes big as if experiencing Sweet Wine Road and its scenery for the first time. He held Place closely and whispered a blessing for all of them, "Que Dios nos bendiga."

Mitch, her window rolled down all the way, looked out and up at the stars. With her free hand, she rubbed Place's thigh gently and looked for the ridge of stars he had once tried to point out to her.